LOVE GONE AWRY

When Sara had first met Abigail, she had to admit, she'd found her stiff and fussy. Then Malcolm MacEwan had come into Abigail's life. Love had softened her rigidity and happiness opened her heart.

Now it seemed Abigail had thrown it all away. Sara couldn't understand why. There was something in this story that just didn't make sense.

The girls hadn't seen Malcolm since the engagement had been broken, but Sara had overheard Mrs. Biggins telling the Lawsons that he was a broken man. She shivered at the image such words brought to mind.

There was no doubt about it. Sara and Felicity simultaneously concurred that it was up to them to contrive some way to reunite Malcolm and Abigail.

Well after they had been sent to bed, the girls still deliberated, sitting huddled under the quilt. They discussed the situation over and over, wondering what they could do. . . .

**Also available in the Road to Avonlea series
from Bantam Skylark Books**

Aunt Abigail's Beau

Storybook written by
Amy Jo Cooper

Based on the Sullivan Films Production
written by Heather Conkie
adapted from the novels of

Lucy Maud Montgomery

A BANTAM SKYLARK BOOK
NEW YORK • TORONTO • LONDON • SYDNEY • AUCKLAND

Based on the Sullivan Films Production produced by Sullivan Films Inc.
in association with CBC and the Disney Channel with the participation of
Telefilm Canada adapted from Lucy Maud Montgomery's novels.

Teleplay written by Heather Conkie.
Copyright © 1989 by Sullivan Films Distribution, Inc.

This edition contains the complete text
of the original edition.
NOT ONE WORD HAS BEEN OMITTED.

RL 6, 008–012

AUNT ABIGAIL'S BEAU

A Bantam Skylark Book / published by arrangement with
HarperCollins Publishers Ltd.

PRINTING HISTORY
HarperCollins edition published 1991
Bantam edition / October 1992

Skylark Books is a registered trademark of Bantam Books,
a division of Bantam Doubleday Dell Publishing Group, Inc.
Registered in U.S. Patent and Trademark Office and elsewhere.

All rights reserved
Storybook written by Amy Jo Cooper.
Copyright © 1991 by HarperCollins Publishers, Sullivan Films
Distribution, Inc., and Ruth Macdonald and David Macdonald.
No part of this book may be reproduced or transmitted
in any form or by any means, electronic or mechanical,
including photocopying, recording, or by any information
storage and retrieval system, without permission in
writing from the publisher.
For information address: HarperCollins Publishers Ltd., Suite 2900,
Hazelton Lanes, 55 Avenue Road, Toronto, Canada M5R 3L2.

ISBN 0-553-48033-2

Bantam Books are published by Bantam Books, a division of Bantam
Doubleday Dell Publishing Group, Inc. Its trademark, consisting of the
words "Bantam Books" and the portrayal of a rooster, is Registered in
U.S. Patent and Trademark Office and in other countries. Marca
Registrada. Bantam Books, 666 Fifth Avenue, New York, New York
10103.

PRINTED IN THE UNITED STATES OF AMERICA

OPM   0 9 8 7 6 5 4 3 2 1

Chapter One

"It's just so..." Sara took a deep breath, knowing the pause would add weight to her pronouncement, "...*romantic*," she breathed with a sigh. Above her, the blue sky spun around. Beneath her, the earth rolled and tilted deliciously. She closed her eyes to savor the feeling.

"I don't think it's romantic at all, Sara Stanley. I think it's rash. I would insist on a proper wedding," Felicity replied, twirling herself round and round until she, too, plopped down in the long grass and surrendered to dizziness. Thirteen-year-old Felicity prided herself on knowing what is, and, what is not, proper.

Sara never paid much mind to the opinions of her cousin. At twelve years old, to elope seemed to Sara the only way to get married. The idea struck her as so exciting, so thrilling, so full of romance that the idea of a regular wedding seemed hardly worth considering at all.

She opened her eyes. The sky had stopped spinning now. Sara watched as a wispy white cloud sailed lazily by. She stretched, and breathed in the sweetness of the grass.

"I want a wedding so I can wear a beautiful dress, just like Mama's," said Cecily who was so dizzy now from turning circles like the older girls that she too fell right down.

Felicity jumped up and started to twirl again. "I want a big wedding, with lots of guests and a party afterwards."

Sara joined her, spinning even faster. "I want a big party, with lots of people, and musicians from Halifax."

"I don't think you're allowed to have a party if you elope," Felicity stated. She was sure she knew the proper etiquette on matters such as this.

"And why ever not? I'm sure it's perfectly allowable," Sara said, even though she *wasn't* exactly sure. "And I would kiss my husband right there, in front of everybody."

"Sara Stanley!" Felicity was so shocked she stopped twirling. "You wouldn't."

Sara, unaware that her cousin had stopped, spun right into her, upending them both. The two girls collapsed in a fit of giggles.

"Just see if I don't," Sara teased, and then she sprawled out flat on the ground and continued to laugh as the sky turned circles above her.

For the whole of that beautiful, late August morning, Sara and Felicity had been examining, in some detail, the topic of love and marriage. What had started the discussion was a story Sara had read in a ladies' magazine about an ill-fated love-match and elopement. The story had, alas, ended tragically, but Sara loved it, and had recounted it all, every last detail, to her cousin Felicity.

This day promised an extra entertainment, too. Sara and Felicity were going over to Aunt Abigail's to help her make her preserves and pickles. It was not that Sara was keen to stand in a steamy kitchen and can fruits and vegetables. Rather, the cause of her great enthusiasm lay in the fact that today she would finally have the chance to meet Miss Abigail Ward.

Abigail Ward was not, strictly speaking, her real aunt. She was Janet King's sister, so she was Sara's aunt only by marriage. Abigail lived on the other side of town in a house reputed to be the cleanest in Avonlea. Sara was most curious to meet this house-keeper extraordinaire, and to see the house that had won the admiration of all the women in the village.

The girls still had the whole morning to spend as they pleased. So, one more time, Sara related the tale of tragic love, embellishing it where she felt it was necessary. And once they had had their fill of romance, the three girls twirled and twirled some more, until the ground rocked beneath them. Then, dizzy with happiness, they trundled back to the King farm for lunch on shaky, wobbly legs.

Neat as a pin—just as a house should be. Abigail Ward took a deep breath. The rich aroma of furniture oil filled her nostrils. It smelled sweeter to her than all the perfumes of Arabia.

While her nieces were twirling themselves dizzy and contemplating love, Abigail Ward was meditating on cleanliness. Dust-rag in hand, she looked around her parlor. The oak floors gleamed richly with their new coat of wax. The doilies, clean and crisp, draped themselves protectively over the backs of the armchairs. Abigail ran her hand over the mahogany table. Her reflection gleamed from its rich, dark surface. She smiled back at herself and patted her ginger hair—not that she really needed to, mind you. Rarely was her hair out of place.

Automatically, she turned her eyes to the portrait over the fireplace. The image of the late Reverend Archibald Ward stared augustly down from his freshly dusted frame. Abigail gave him a timid smile. Then, straightening her already smooth skirt, she fluttered into the kitchen to prepare for the arrival of her nieces.

Chapter Two

With lunch now finished at the King farm, Sara sat at the old pine table in the kitchen. Scattered before her were old family photographs. The morning's conversation had continued through the meal and had given Felicity the notion to dig up her parents' wedding pictures.

"Wasn't mother's wedding dress beautiful?" Felicity sighed.

Sara took the photograph from her cousin's hands and gazed at the graceful young girl shyly holding her bouquet. Indeed, it *was* beautiful. The shiny white satin fitted her elegantly and flowed smoothly down, pooling in a wide swirl at her feet. Her fair tresses, neatly coiffed, were covered with a soft veil of the most exquisite lace. Its delicate weave made Sara think of the intricate designs of a spider's web or the gossamer wings of fairies.

The King kitchen was a cozy room, and the customary activity and confusion of the family bustled all around Sara as she studied the photograph. She was accustomed to the commotion now. She was able to slip into it the way one would a favorite old sweater.

She hadn't felt so comfortable, when she'd first arrived in Avonlea. Her father had sent her from Montreal, after false accusations caused his business to falter and his reputation to be questioned. Sara was to live with her late mother's family until he sorted out his affairs. Though she was living at nearby Rose Cottage with her Aunt Hetty and Aunt Oliva, she spent much of her time with her cousins at the King farm. As the only child of a widower, Sara was not used to the hustle and bustle of a large family life, but time and familiarity worked their charms, and she was soon caught up in its whirlwind of warmth and affection.

The late morning sun streamed through the large kitchen window, gracing each thing it touched with its soft, golden fingers. A big soup pot bubbled away on the cast-iron stove. Beside it, Aunt Janet stirred and chopped, fussing and fixing.

Quite often, Aunt Janet was the source of much of the bustle and confusion in the King household. She reminded Sara of the big, white mother hen out in the farmyard who was constantly clucking and worrying her brood into line. Janet delivered a steady stream of advice, most of which went unheeded by her family, if only because there was always so much of it.

Sara watched her aunt. There was a soft, plump hominess to Janet now, so different from the slender and demure young woman in the portrait. Sara recalled a few lonely nights when, new to the place and aching with homesickness, she had found solace in the wide lap of that big-hearted woman.

"Hadn't you two better get going?" Aunt Janet asked. "Abigail said noon, and you know how she likes you to be punctual."

Felicity jumped up, clapped her hands in glee and ran eagerly to get her sweater.

"Really, Felicity." Sara spoke in what Aunt Hetty called her "Queen of England" tone. "I cannot understand how you can get so excited about putting little bits of fruit and vegetables into jars and sticking them in a cold, dingy cellar."

"Well," huffed Felicity, who could sound just as imperious, "that's just because you've never done it before, Sara Stanley. *My* preserves are just as good as any grown-up's. That's why Aunt Abigail asked for me especially."

"Perhaps you're right, dear." Janet remarked. "But I suspect Abigail asked for you because *I* refused to do it. My sister," she said, rolling her eyes heavenward, "has a definite method of doing things, and woe betide anyone who dares try doing it her own way."

Felicity had to agree. "She *can* be a little fussy at times."

"Clemmie Ray's mother says she's a dyed-in-old-wool maid." Cecily, her mouth full of cookie and words, stumbled over this bit of information.

Janet laughed, her face softening with love for her youngest child. "You mean dyed-in-the-wool old maid."

Felicity pursed her lips, and with a knowing air, remarked, "Well, she never did marry, Mother."

"Maybe she had the good sense she was born with," Alec quipped from the plump old armchair where he sat nestled with a book.

Janet's face twitched slightly. Her smile disappeared. His words seemed to hurt her.

"She got used to her own way, that's all. We all do as we get older."

Felicity, who, like her mother, often had an opinion of her own, felt it her duty to comment.

"I think it's terrible to get set in your ways when you're old."

"Is that why you did it while you were still young, Felicity?" her father teased. Sara hid her face to stifle her smile.

Felicity huffed, but she was determined not to be goaded. There existed between father and daughter the type of teasing that often occurs between two people of similar natures. They see in the other that which they can't abide in themselves.

"She comes by it honestly, Alec King," Janet reproached. It was his slow, even temperament that had first attracted her to her husband, but she knew, all too well, how that same steadiness could dig in its heels and turn to stubbornness.

Like an ostrich in the sand, Alec buried his head in his book. His wife's remark stung him, striking a sore point. I won't give her the satisfaction, he thought. His silence spoke loudly.

A certain uneasiness settled over the room, an uneasiness reflected in the unusually hesitant tone in Janet's next question.

"Alec, could you, uh, drop the girls off on your way over?"

Alec stared at her, thoroughly perplexed.

"On my way where?"

"Mrs. Lloyd's!" Janet almost gasped in her exasperation. "I told her you'd deliver her eggs, remember?"

Snap—the book shut. Slowly and deliberately, Alec King removed his wire-rimmed reading glasses and put them away carefully in their case. Sara's arm, halfway in her sweater and halfway out, hung, suspended. Cecily forgot her fidgeting. Everyone waited.

Each word dropped in equal measure.

"I wish, just once, someone would consult with

me before they volunteer my services." Then, perhaps to soften the force of his words, or, perhaps in explanation, Alec added in defense, "I do have things to do, you know."

Janet's eyebrow shot up faster than a rabbit at the sound of the hounds. Her nostrils flared, and her two chins quivered and quaked in anger. "Oh?" she responded. "Things like fixing our bed instead of burying your nose in a book?" Janet never could stop once she had built up a head of steam. "That leg is so wobbly, we're going to wake up on the floor one of these nights."

Felicity whined rather impatiently. "Father, please hurry up. Aunt Abigail will be cross, and then she'll spoil the whole afternoon."

With an audible sigh barely masking his displeasure, Alec King heaved himself from his chair.

"All right, Felicity, hold your horses."

Without as much as a word or glance towards his wife, Alec King made his way to the crowded little vestibule off the kitchen where the family hung their coats and kicked off their muddy boots.

"Well, someone's in a bad mood," Janet commented. She was never one to let a remark remain unsaid. It was an unfortunate habit.

Alec King did not deign to reply. His coat was on and he was almost out the door before his wife called him back.

"Alec, don't forget the eggs."

Pressing his lips together, Alec silently retrieved the basket.

Hurt by his silence and confused by his manner, Janet complained, "Sometimes I think you deliberately don't listen."

A steady stare, more eloquent than words, was his only reply. Turning his back, he stomped out the door.

Sara hurriedly kissed Aunt Janet goodbye and followed after her uncle. Felicity kissed her twice, as if to make up for the kiss she knew her mother had desired, but hadn't received.

Chapter Three

The late summer day held great promise of something, though Sara couldn't quite tell what. It was more of a feeling, a vague sensation—nothing she could put her finger on. In the fields they passed, the crops were abundant, ready for the harvest. The odd tree had already donned its scarlet autumn cloak, as if it, too, expected something special to happen. The whole world seemed poised in anticipation of...Sara did not know what.

Throughout the short journey, Felicity chattered on, expressing her opinions on a variety of topics, from canning to matters matrimonial. The patter of her words competed with the clatter of the wheels as the buggy made its way towards town. It was almost as if she felt it were her duty to make up for the silence of the others.

Sara, whose imagination often took her to worlds other than her own, understood that a mind sometimes needs to escape for a while, but Uncle Alec seemed so far away, even though he was sitting right next to her driving the buggy. His soft brown eyes stared ahead, lost in thought. His eyes had the same gentleness that gazed out at her from the cherished photograph she kept of her mother, Alec's younger sister. They were King family eyes: gentle, thoughtful, but stubborn if they chose to be. Was there something wrong?

Gingerly, Sara touched her uncle's sleeve. He stirred himself from his reverie, cocked his head slightly and gave her a quick wink. His brief smile held a touch of sadness.

"I think that it's perfectly dreadful that poor Aunt Abigail never married." A sharp voice from the back cut through Sara's thoughts.

"Maybe she just never found the right fellow," her father countered with a wry smile.

"But she could have. Mother said so." Once Felicity had snatched hold of a topic, there was no letting go.

"She's too set in her ways to marry now," Alec said with a finality that put an end to the discussion.

The buggy made its gentle way through Avonlea and turned along a well-worn path. A few houses, respectable in bearing, perched primly along the road. Set off slightly from the rest, aloof but not distant, sat the domain of the late Reverend Archibald Ward.

Even on the outside, it was the cleanest house Sara had ever seen. Its white paint gleamed spotlessly, like a face freshly scrubbed. On the smooth, green lawn, not one blade of grass was out of place. Flowers bloomed dutifully in their tidy beds, not daring to step out of their orderly rows. Bright, yellow marigolds lined up in front, followed by scarlet geraniums, with the taller delphiniums obediently behind. Everything about the modest cottage was neat and proper.

Alec had barely stopped the buggy before the girls jumped off. With a quick wave goodbye, they scurried through the gate—Felicity made sure she closed it behind her—and up the porch steps.

A small, black metal dog stood sentinel by the bright red door, and, without stopping to think, Felicity scraped first one shoe, then the next against its sharp back. Sara stared in amazement. It was the most curious thing.

"What are you doing?"

"It's a scraper. Use it," Felicity ordered.

Sara regarded the metal dog with a mixture of awe and confusion. With sightless eyes, it glared out at the world. Its cast-iron muzzle was set, defying anyone to bring just the slightest speck of dust into the house.

"But my shoes aren't dirty."

"It doesn't matter." Felicity rapped twice on the door, as if to emphasize her point, "You're not to set foot in Aunt Abigail's front hall unless you've scraped your feet." Felicity's haughty air turned confidential. She leaned forward slightly and lowered her voice. "She's very particular, you know." Felicity straightened her sweater and smoothed back her hair.

Sara expected an ogre to answer the door. The yellow wildflowers she had picked that morning suddenly seemed improper. Why hadn't she clipped some roses from Aunt Hetty's garden? They were much neater. She looked around hurriedly for a place to discreetly dump the unwanted bouquet, but she was too late.

"Hello, Felicity dear. Hello, Sara." A voice, whose sweet tones held within them an edge of sharpness, greeted them. A trim, pleasant-looking woman stood in the doorway.

Abigail Ward was as tidy as her house. Her slim figure was dressed unassumingly in a plain blouse and skirt, starched and neat. There was nothing frilly about Abigail. The ginger tones in her red hair complemented the ruddiness of her well-scrubbed cheeks. A tight smile darted across her face.

"I've been meaning to have you over for such a long time, Sara dear. It's good of you to come."

With no place else to deposit her flowers, Sara was forced to offer her gift.

"These are for you."

Aunt Abigail graciously accepted the bouquet. With nimble and experienced fingers, she straightened out the unruly bunch, plucking out the odd wilted flower and making the stems all even, taming their former wildness.

"Thank you, Sara. Now come along," she urged, and she turned on her heels and flitted into the house. There was nothing else to do but follow.

Chapter Four

Sara stepped tentatively onto the polished floor. The air was redolent with the bittersweet smell of furniture polish. She wrinkled her nose.

"Cozy" did not exactly describe this house. Although it was spotless, with gleaming woodwork, and tastefully arranged furniture, there was a certain unbending rigidness that was less than welcoming.

"Come in, come in." Abigail inhaled the fragrance of the bouquet, her eyes tightly closed. "These are lovely," she murmured, then, snapping into efficiency, "I must find something to put them in."

"How about this vase?" Sara lifted a delicate porcelain vase from its carefully chosen position on the hallway table.

Blue eyes popping in horror, Abigail politely swooped and seized the precious object from Sara's hand. "Oh no." Her voice shot up one octave, and then scaled itself down. "That's Aunt Tessa's vase." Carefully, she replaced the cherished heirloom to its proper position. "Wouldn't do to use that." She adjusted the vase just a fraction to the left, then twirled smartly and faced the girls, relieved that order had been restored. Abigail brushed a bit of fluff from Sara's sweater and smiled sweetly. "We'll find an everyday vase in the kitchen. Come along," she ordered. Brandishing the flowers overhead, she advanced towards the kitchen. Her skirt flapped and snapped around her as she disappeared through the door.

Felicity looked at Sara. Sara, eyes wide with amazement, returned her cousin's gaze. They shrugged their shoulders and followed in their aunt's wake.

For most of her life, Abigail Ward had lived a life of duty. She'd been only seventeen when her mother died, and two months before the sad death of her beloved parent, her sister Janet, older by three years, had married young Alec King. As Abigail was the only other child, it fell to her to be her father's housekeeper. With a willing obedience, she'd accepted her role. Her father's care and comfort became her major concern. When duty called, Abigail had not been afraid to answer.

The Reverend Ward was a learned but difficult man. To his congregation, he was a true shepherd, leading them straight along the paths of righteousness. To his daughters, he was a loving, if not over strict, parent. Archibald Ward did not believe in spoiling his children with unnecessary affection.

The Reverend Ward had his standards, and Abigail strove hard to meet them. For ten years she served him, cooking and cleaning. Through all those long years, she remained a cheerful companion and helpmate.

When the Reverend Ward passed on from this earthly life and went to reap his heavenly rewards, Abigail continued living a life of duty and service. With no one left to take care of, she directed her selfless energies towards helping the community. Each spring she sewed a quilt for the church ladies auxiliary. Through the long winter nights she knitted stockings for the Widows' and Orphans' Fund. Late summer was the time for her famous preserves.

The strawberries bubbling on the stove gave off a warm, sweet fragrance. Abigail stood over the tall pot, stirring the thick, sticky mixture. Tendrils of hair, moistened from the steam, fell softly about her face. Her's had been a good life, she thought to herself. And if it had been a trifle lonely, Abigail would never have admitted it. Although, there was a time...the wistful thought rose up with the steam from the pot. Abigail pressed the wooden spoon into the strawberries, as if to squash down an intruding memory.

Orderly piles of sweet pears, juicy tomatoes and green, warty cucumbers waited patiently to be transformed into preserves and pickles. Empty mason jars, boiled spotless, stood at attention on the maplewood sideboard. Pots burbled and bubbled on the gleaming white stove. Sara tried to remember the detailed instructions Aunt Abigail had given her. Never before had she heard so many "do's" and "don't's." Wearing a pristinely clean and starched apron, Sara was afraid to move lest she bump into and break one of Abigail's rules.

"Even though I *did* win the junior category at the fair last year, Aunt Abigail, I'm sure to learn something from such an expert as yourself." Felicity prattled on happily as she skilfully peeled and sliced some pears. She was perfectly at home in the spotless kitchen and at ease with the task at hand.

Abigail smiled indulgently towards her niece. "Oh, I'm no expert, Felicity. To me it's just a job that needs to be done. If people didn't expect me to make preserves every year, I probably wouldn't."

"But you win the ribbon every year."

Abigail humbly brushed off the remark with a wave of her hand. There was no room in her life for vanity.

"Ribbons?" she queried. "What am I to do with ribbons?" But deep inside, a warm sense of pride tingled and glowed, causing a faint blush to color her cheeks. It was a momentary feeling, one she quickly extinguished. "Many hands make light work," she explained, "and I enjoy your company."

Peeling pears was not something that came naturally to Sara. More often than not, big chunks of the juicy, white fruit fell off with the thin, yellow peel, and many were the pieces that landed on the floor.

She watched with some envy as Felicity neatly trimmed a pear. The peel came off all in one piece and coiled itself on the table. Sara applied her knife and, in direct imitation, tried to copy her cousin's movements. A strip of yellow skin unwound itself as Sara carefully pared. An unfortunate flick of her knife severed the peel from the fruit. Instead of dropping on the table, the disobedient paring leapt from the knife and soared gracefully to the floor. Disappointed, Sara tried again.

"Sara, please don't let those peelings fall on the floor."

Although her aunt's tone was meant to be pleasant, Sara felt a shock of shame at the reprimand. It had been her intention to pick up all the peelings once her task was done. She had *not*—she hoped Miss Ward understood—been raised in a barn. Her embarrassment wasn't helped by Felicity's smirk and the superior way she pointed her nose in the air.

Hurriedly, Sara snatched a cloth from the table. "I'm sorry, I'll clean it up." She dropped quickly to the floor in an effort to prove to Aunt Abigail that she, too, knew the virtue of cleanliness. Before she had time to apply the cloth, her movements were arrested by her aunt's alarm.

"Oh, don't use *that* cloth. That's for the dishes," she explained, in that precise, slightly louder voice people usually use for foreigners and those slow of wit. "I never use that cloth on the floor."

Just then, a knock at the front door made everyone pause. A puzzled frown played on Abigail's brow. Pausing only to replace a chair that had strayed from the table, Abigail walked briskly to the door.

It was wicked of her, she knew, but Sara just couldn't resist. She never liked to feel that she had made a mistake. Abigail's rebuke still smarted, and the memory of her embarrassment rose up again. How was she to know that cloth was for the dishes?

Raising her hands in the air in mock astonishment, then shaking her finger, Sara scolded a chair for being out of line. Taking it firmly in hand, she hustled the errant chair back to its place, exaggerating her aunt's fussy movements. Neither girl tried to hide their giggles.

A loud crash, followed by a shriek from Aunt Abigail, made them stop their laughter and catch their breath.

Chapter Five

As she'd approached the door, Abigail was more than a little alarmed. She never received callers at this time of the day. There was no one she was expecting. People didn't usually just drop by. What if it were news of some dreadful tragedy? The mere idea had set her heart pounding.

Caution slowed her progress. Her fingers flew unthinkingly to the plain gold watch-pin that hung on her blouse, close to her heart. With unseeing eyes, she checked the time. She composed herself and opened the door.

Was it a ghost? Her heart leapt to her throat in alarm. It was too solid to be a mere apparition. Her mouth opened for what seemed an eternity before she could find her voice.

"Is it really you? Malcolm MacEwan?"

A thousand different emotions assailed her. A rush of memories, many sweet and some very bitter, all sprang up at once. The very force of the remembrance made her dizzy.

With all the grace of a lumbering bull, Malcolm MacEwan charged through the threshold and swept Abigail Ward into his eager arms. The white daisies he had picked as a gift scattered as, in the excess of his joy, he twirled his beloved around in a passionate embrace, almost as if they were living a scene from a romantic novel.

Unfortunately, Abigail had been totally unprepared for the onslaught. Soft, cooing words are usually called for, but the surprise attack elicited from her a shriek of such a pitch that it could possibly, under the right conditions, have woken the dead.

Instead of melting willingly against the manly chest of her sweetheart, as would have been the proper thing, Abigail, caught completely off guard, merely stiffened. Her legs stuck out straight as flagpoles. As he swung her around, her boots careened into the small rattan table that held her favorite fern. Dirt flew everywhere. Her foremost thought as Mr. MacEwan spun with her in his arms for a second time was, "I must get a broom."

She landed clumsily, with legs and arms slightly akimbo. She recovered, as did Malcolm. Awkwardly, each took up a position, an appropriate distance from each other. Both were overcome by a sudden shyness. Remembering his manners, Malcolm quickly yanked the tweed cap from his head and held it crushed respectably against his heart.

"Are you surprised to see me after all these years?" His deep voice lilted with a Scottish brogue. "Let's not count how many."

"Well, it's seven years this November," she sweetly reminded him. Not that she had been counting.

It was the same dear face she had loved and had missed so much, only older. His lank brown hair was now sprinkled with gray. There were a few lines etched around his eyes and at the corners of his mouth, but they only made him more handsome. His hazel eyes still shone with an eagerness to please. She recalled how he would moon after her with those puppy eyes, following her home from school. The mustache was new. She wasn't sure if it suited him.

"You haven't changed a bit, Abby." He stared at her fondly, drinking in her loveliness like a parched man at a well. Then, remembering his purpose, he cleared his throat and addressed her formally. He had been practicing these lines for seven years.

"Yukon gold has made me a rich man, and I'd like to renew our acquaintance. If you're not already hitched, that is."

"If I'm not wha—? Oh! Oh, no, Mr. Mac—"
Flustered, she colored with a young maiden's blush.
"No. That is, I'm not married."

"Hallelujah. Ah, but it is good to see you again."

The girls' first thought when they heard their
aunt scream, was that someone, perhaps a maniac,
had attacked their aunt. They'd listened carefully,
but no other sounds issued from the hall. It was Sara
who had finally decided they should investigate.

Quietly, they made their way from the kitchen
to the front hall. Felicity tightened her grip on the
paring knife she had decided to carry as an extra
precaution, in case bravery was called for. Sara
managed to swing open the kitchen door without
so much as a creak.

A maniac would have been less surprising than
what they actually saw. A man—a large, ruggedly
handsome man, dressed in a fine, if not exactly
tasteful, plaid suit—kissing Aunt Abigail! His head
bobbed like a chicken as he quickly pecked her on
the forehead, and then on both cheeks.

A soft gurgle emerged from Felicity's wide-open
mouth. For a second, it looked as though she might
have been struck speechless. Fortunately, she was
able to recover. Vaguely waving her knife, as if to
illustrate her point, Felicity hesitantly managed,
"Aunt Abigail. We've...we've finished chopping."

What a different Abigail turned to meet them. Her complexion glowed. The usually sharp angles of her face had softened to a pleasing loveliness. Her stiff little smile relaxed to a happy grin that spread unchecked across her face. The rigid bun that had always sat severely atop her head had slipped and floated down to one side like a ship loosed from its moorings.

She pretended not to notice the astonished faces, the small kitchen knife held aloft. Acting as if she always had strange men in her hallway, Abigail, only slightly perturbed, made the introductions, mustering up as much of her hostess skills as were possible in such a situation.

"Malcolm, I'd like you to meet Sara Stanley. She's staying with us here in Avonlea from Montreal." Sara, still somewhat in shock, gave a quick little nod. "And perhaps you remember Felicity, my sister Janet's daughter. Girls, this is Mr. Malcolm MacEwan."

"Glad to meet you, Sara. Felicity, I would never have recognized you. Why, you were just a wee thing."

There was an uncomfortable moment as everyone just stood there, smiling. It was only broken when Abigail, aware suddenly that all around her was chaos, ducked down quickly to gather the flowers strewn around her hall.

"I picked those for you on my way over." Malcolm, his manners suddenly occurring to him, dropped down to assist.

Sara and Felicity watched in amazement as the two adults bobbed and weaved for the scattered blooms. They moved like puppets jerking about on strings. Several times they just missed knocking their heads together.

Malcolm held up the reassembled bouquet. "Where would you like me to put 'em? Oh, this will do." With a sure and decisive stride he advanced upon the hall table and crammed the flowers down the unsuspecting throat of Aunt Tessa's vase.

Shock inhabited every one of Abigail's features. Sara and Felicity waited with baited breath for the outcome. Abigail blinked back her dismay, and, with a forced enthusiasm, she smiled.

"Ah, a prettier vase there never was." Malcolm was pleased with himself. "I apologize, young ladies. I don't mean to be rude, but if you don't mind, I'd like to have a wee moment with your aunt alone."

Felicity barely had time to deposit the paring knife on the table before being escorted gently out the door by Malcolm MacEwan.

"Goodbye, Aunt Abigail." Felicity turned to get one last peek at her aunt as she was tenderly nudged through the threshold.

"Nice to meet you, Mr. MacEwan." Sara dropped what she hoped was a smart curtsy, then followed quickly after her cousin.

Chapter Six

Sara and Felicity fairly flew from Aunt Abigail's house, across the field rich with its golden wheat. Sara plopped down on the ground and lay on her back, hidden by the rustling stalks. The sun warmed her face and the wheat tickled her skin. A story began to form in her mind: story of lovers, cruelly separated and sorely tested; of love that remained pure even through the trials of absence; of lovers, happily united, their love enduring forever.

Felicity dropped down beside her. Some chaff clung to her hair. Her eyes were shiny with laughter. Spontaneously, they both broke out into another rash of giggles. It was the third attack since leaving Abigail's. How romantic it all was! How wonderfully handsome he was. How absolutely silly Abigail looked with her hair all askew and her clothes all mussed!

"Now that," Sara said, choking back her mirth, "is what my Nanny Louisa would call 'a fine specimen of a man.' "

Since Felicity had little experience of such

things, she had to agree. "Oh, poor Aunt Abigail," she sighed wistfully, for she was sure that being wistful was the proper emotion in such matters.

"Poor Great-aunt Tessa's vase!"

"And did you ever see such kisses?" It had shocked Felicity, and the memory still caused her to blush.

A dramatic light gleamed in Sara's eye. Grabbing her cousin by both arms, she intoned in her best Scottish accent, "If you don't mind, lassies, I'd like to have a wee moment with your aunt," Sara raised her eyebrow to add significance, "on my own."

Before she knew what had hit her, Felicity received three kisses, smack on her cheek.

"Sara, oh, yech!"

Sara jumped up and ran swishing through the field.

"Sara," Felicity called before chasing after her. "I can't wait to tell Mother and Father."

Seven long years ago, without a word, without an explanation, Malcolm MacEwan had left Avonlea. The agony his departure caused nearly broke Abigail's heart. It was only by chance that she heard the news, for Malcolm had sent her no letter, had given her no explanation of his leaving. The pain of it grieved her to the center of her being.

She could remember exactly how she'd felt

when she first heard the news. She had been ordering some muslin in Lawson's general store. Four yards—she could recall the measure exactly. It was Mrs. Potts who had let the information drop. The force of the words rocked her so violently, that, at first, she thought an earthquake had hit the village. Recovering, she looked around. Why was no one else shaken? Behind her, someone hissed at Mrs. Potts to hush. Everyone stared at her with eyes just as curious as they were sympathetic.

But Abigail was determined not to let anyone know her sorrow. With a cheerful demeanor that belied the suffering within, she went about her business. So convincing was she, that it became common gossip that it was the prim Abigail Ward who had broken the poor heart of Malcolm MacEwan, instead of the other way around. From that day on, her devotion to outward appearances increased; no one knew that it was to cover up a heart broken inside.

For several years after his departure, Abigail nursed a fantasy of his return. Every night, as she lay in bed, she planned in her mind exactly how it would occur. One fine day he would walk up the road, through the gate, along the path and up the stairs to the door. Masterfully, he would knock. "Who could that be?" she would think to herself. Setting down her duster, she would answer the door. How surprised she would be to see him! But she would never let him see her happiness. Oh no. She would remain calm, distant, even a bit icy in her greeting.

After scraping his feet, he would enter. Only when he had begged her forgiveness on bended knee and avowed his undying love for her would she relent. Then, in a simple ceremony, they would marry, living happily and in harmony until the end of their lives.

For many years her little dream sweetened her existence, and she clung to it as a drowning person does a life preserver. But, as the years advanced and he didn't return or write to her, her hope turned to bitterness. As she grew older, she realized it for what it was—a girlish fantasy. It made her blush to think that she could possibly have held on to such a frivolous dream. She accepted that he was gone from her life. It was foolish to think otherwise.

But, now, Malcolm MacEwan had returned.

Chapter Seven

"Put it on, put it on," Malcolm urged her eagerly. His large frame shook the fragile parlor chair.

Ten pear-shaped garnets dropped like tears from a thick gold chain. It was so—Abigail tried hard to think of the correct word—ornate. She preferred much simpler adornment.

"I'm not accustomed to such...extravagant jewellery, Mr. MacEwan."

Mistaking her reluctance for modesty, Malcolm scooped the heavy ornament from her hands and placed it around her neck. The dear lass is overwhelmed, he reasoned. She was always like that. Never expecting anything for herself, always giving to others. Well, he thought with great pleasure, I'll soon change that.

"I'll buy you a present a day, if it'll make you happy," he said, sweeping his arm in wide enthusiasm as if to encompass the great wealth of his love. Unfortunately, the small table sitting beside his chair fell victim to his zeal. With a soft thud, it hit the carpet. The delicate teacup which had, until that moment, sat innocently perched on its polished surface followed quickly behind. The tea spread quickly, leaving its brown stain on the blues and reds of the oriental carpet.

Up popped Abigail. In a flash, she was on her knees with a cloth trying her best to mop up the tea. Embarrassed by his clumsiness and feeling it incumbent upon him to act, Malcolm, too, jumped up. Awkwardly, he flung his arms about in futile gestures of assistance.

"I'm sorry. Here, let me wipe it up. How clumsy

can a man be?" As if in answer to his own question, his foot collided with the upturned table .

"Please," her voice sang with careful control, "please sit down, Mr. MacEwan."

Obeying, he plunked himself down. The chair groaned under the suddenness of his weight. They sat for a few minutes in an embarrassed silence.

"I'm sorry, Abby. I'm not good at this sort of thing. There's a whole lot I'm not used to. You might have to help me out a bit with my p's and q's."

The humble sincerity of his apology softened her heart.

"No harm done. I should have remembered that you were all thumbs."

"I'm sorry, too, if I bowled you over a bit. It's just that I've never been so pleased to see somebody again in my whole life."

"Well, I've never been so surprised to see someone, Mr. MacEwan." She was confused by the edge of bitterness that sharpened her tone.

"Call me Malcolm, Abby. You're making me feel like a stranger."

"Well, you are quite a stranger to me, Mr. MacEwan. It has been seven years this November twenty-third."

"I know, and I'm not willing to let any more time slip through my fingers."

They both seemed to feel it at once—the steely

glance glaring down from the portrait above. Malcolm shifted uncomfortably.

"Blast it if your father's eyes don't follow me around just like they used to when he sat in this very chair."

With boldness he would never have dared before, Malcolm confronted the image of the dour old man.

"I've shown you, haven't I, you old cuss. You refused my proposal. 'Come back, Malcolm, when you're rich. Then you can marry Abigail.'"

Pleased with himself, Malcolm faced Abigail and continued.

"He thought it was a safe bet. I did it, though. It took a while, but I did it."

The question she had been longing to ask, the question that had been buried in her heart for years, came softly to her lips.

"Why did you leave so suddenly, without so much as a word?" The old pain stabbed her with a renewed sharpness. "Didn't you know how that would make me feel?"

His chest, puffed out in defiance, suddenly deflated. His honest features couldn't hide his remorse. Quietly he confessed, "I'm ashamed of that, and I'm sorry. But there was no time. I wanted to make something of myself, to make you proud of me. And all the while, it was thinking of you that kept me going. And here you are, sitting right across from me."

His words were a salve to her sore heart. Joy brought tears to her eyes. It was only with much blinking that she was able to keep them back. A lightness she had not felt in a long, long time brightened her soul.

"Abby." His voice was gentle. "Do you remember how we felt about each other?"

Memories of long-buried feelings made her blush.

"Yes." And with that word came a barely audible sigh.

"Well, uh, can I..." He quickly corrected himself. "...may I come calling again?"

Old habits die hard. Without thinking, Abigail's eyes darted quickly towards the portrait of her father, as if seeking permission. Malcolm followed her gaze. Sensing her unease, he took the matter in hand.

Adopting a formal stance, Malcolm positioned himself before the image of the late Archibald Ward. No more would he have to feel humble in front of the man who had treated him so unfairly. Clearing his throat, and in tones he hoped would convey the respect he did not feel, he addressed the portrait.

"Reverend Ward, sir. I'm rich. You've always been a man of your word. May I now come courting your daughter, Abigail?" He felt a bit ridiculous, talking to a painting. But, a woman's fancies were a mysterious thing. It was what Abby desired. He loved her so much, he would go to the end of the world and back if she ordered it.

"He said 'yes.' What do *you* say?" He turned to her.

Abigail smiled. Dear old Malcolm.

"Yes, yes, you may..." She then spoke aloud the name she had pining to say these seven, inter-minable years. "...Malcolm."

Chapter Eight

Abigail walked through the town proudly on Malcolm's arm. The day was crisp and fine. The sky was a bright blue, and in the warm breeze one could smell the coolness of the approaching fall. Men tipped their hats and women nodded their greetings as the couple strolled along, linked in their happiness. Abigail could not ever remember a more wonderful day.

Malcolm MacEwan's arrival was the biggest news to hit Avonlea since the time that Ian MacEachern, in a fit of pique, rammed his head into a wall and was stuck there for four hours.

The whole town was abuzz with speculation.

"I saw Abigail Ward out strolling with that man, and she looked like the cat who swallowed the canary." Mrs. Biggins had barely placed both feet in the door before she made her announcement to the customers and staff of Lawson's general store.

"Well, I suppose she realizes she's lucky to be courting at all at this late date," Mrs. Potts sharpened her claws. Her feline nature always showed itself when it came to gossip.

Mrs. Biggins could not contain her excitement. "He's got money, to boot. Why, he paid me his entire month's room and board in advance."

"Oh, he's got money all right," Mr. Lawson drawled authoritatively. "Real interested in finding property. He wants a big house."

"And a brood to boot," Mrs. Lawson added, giggling at her own boldness.

"Abigail's no spring chicken. She'd better hurry up if she wants children," came the considered opinion of Mrs. Biggins.

Mrs. Potts's eyes bugged out with the seriousness of her of her next sentiment. "Well, all I can say is, I hope his manners have improved with time. Although the Yukon hardly seems like any kind of finishing school." She pursed her lips and nodded her head.

The tinkling of the bell over the door announced their arrival. As they entered the Lawson's store, Abigail could see, out of the corner of her eye, Mrs. Lawson gesture for silence. She felt her face becoming warm. Abigail knew that everyone had been talking about her. Swallowing her chagrin, she tried to keep her voice even.

"Good morning, Mr. Lawson, Mrs. Lawson."

"Abigail."

There's Mrs. Biggins, and that nosy Mrs. Potts, Abigail realized with a sinking feeling. She managed a sweet smile.

"Morning ladies."

Mrs. Potts' round eyes peered at Abigail. Her pudgy face moulded itself into what she meant to be a smile. Mrs. Biggins acknowledged the greeting with a knowing look, accompanied by a slight flaring of her thin nostrils.

At that moment, Malcolm was overome with pride and affection, and he could not stop himself from planting a big kiss on his beloved's cheek.

"Malcolm!" Abigail squawked. "People are looking."

"Let 'em watch, Abby," Malcolm boomed.

Cavalierly, Malcolm removed a large cigar from his mouth, hurled it to the floor and crushed it, mercilessly, with the heel of his boot.

Abby was mortified. She pounced on the remains of the cigar like a cat on a mouse. The feathers in the hats of the Mrs. Potts and Mrs. Biggins nodded in sympathy, as if to say, "Poor Abigail."

Why was Malcolm behaving this way? People would think him a boor and a braggart. Abigail's embarrassment made her eyes sting.

"Morning, Mr. Lawson, Mrs. Lawson. How do you do, ladies? Why, surrounded by all this female beauty, it's just like walking into a flower garden," Malcolm bowed gallantly.

Mrs. Biggins twittered from behind her lace glove. Mrs. Potts sidled over and extended her plump hand as if she were a duchess.

"Charmed, I'm sure," she cooed, "It's been such a long time, Mr. MacEwan. We were afeared something might have happened to you." Her sarcasm, lost on Malcolm, was not wasted on Abigail.

Malcolm gallantly kissed the proffered hand. With his chest stuck out like the cock-o'-the-walk, he strutted to the counter.

"What can I do for you, Mr. MacEwan?"

"Well, Mr. Lawson, Abby here thinks I need a new suit. I've never had the time of day for all these high, starched collars, but there's no arguing with a lassie once she's made up her mind. Now, what is it you've got for me to see?"

Mr. Lawson scratched his head. "I've some fine ready-made ones, but I'm not sure I happen to have one in your size."

"That might just be the excuse I've been looking for, Mr. Lawson." Malcolm gave him a hearty slap on the back. Mr. Lawson set his glasses back on the bridge of his nose from where they had been dislodged and gestured for Malcolm to follow.

"Oh, by the way." Malcolm stopped short as if he had just remembered his real purpose. "We're also having a bit of a get-together, aren't we Abby?"

Painfully aware that all eyes were focused on her, Abigail attempted a weak little smile. Why did he have to talk so loudly?

"So, we'll be needing some provisions, Mrs. Lawson." With a lordly air, Malcolm looked around.

"We'd like..." Abigail began.

"I'd like five pounds of your best chocolate." With a flourish of his hand, Malcolm delivered his order. Then he rocked back on his heels as pleased as punch. No more would the people of Avonlea see him as poor Malcolm MacEwan.

He must not have heard me, Abigail reasoned to herself. Otherwise, he would not have been so rude as to interrupt. I will have a brief word with him later on the subject.

Much to her relief, Malcolm left the room before he could embarrass her any further.

"A party? Aren't you afraid of dirtying your floors, Abigail?" Mrs. Potts asked, as smooth as honey and just as sticky.

"It's not really a party. Just a small meal for my sister Janet and her family." Abigail chose to ignore the sarcasm. Malcolm truly is a good man, she wanted to tell them. His manners may be rough, but his heart is good. Guilt over her own uneasiness made the need to defend Malcolm all the more pressing. She'd put those old busybodies in their place. She was just about to give them a piece of her mind when the pity in Mrs. Biggins' eyes and the smugness in Mrs. Potts' smile made her painfully aware of how it must all appear.

She blushed.

It was a great relief when Mrs. Lawson had wrapped the chocolates, and she was able to slip out of the store, leaving Malcolm to the purchase of his new clothes.

Chapter Nine

The inhabitants of Avonlea were not the only ones speculating on the courting of Abigail Ward by Malcolm MacEwan. It was the cause of endless discussion at the King farm, especially among the younger, female members of the clan.

To Sara, it was the most romantic thing that could possibly have happened. The story of the tragic separation and happy reunion of Aunt Abigail and Malcolm was one that she told herself at least once a day. And with each telling, a new detail would find its way in, so that after four days, with much embroidery and added filigree, the tale ranked as one of the greatest love stories of all times.

Felicity was thrilled that her poor Aunt Abigail finally had a beau. Perhaps there would be a wedding. How wonderful that would be. Felicity whiled away long, dreamy afternoons making elaborate plans in her mind—details of dress and floral arrangements. All the preparations had to be just so.

They talked so much about this Mr. MacEwan that even Felicity's brother, eleven-year-old Felix, was curious to meet him. Not that he cared so about all that mushy business, but the words "Yukon," "gold" and "adventure" made him prick up his ears and listen. He and his older cousin, Andrew King, who, like Sara, had been sent to the Island to stay with his relatives, would play endless games of bravery and adventure, all based on their slim knowledge of what life must be like in the rugged North.

The day arrived when everyone would finally have their chance to meet Malcolm MacEwan. Abigail had invited the King family, along with their cousins, Sara Stanley and Andrew King, to a dinner party. It promised to be a great event.

Sara took great care that evening with her dress. She tried to look her best for any occasion, but she wanted to look especially nice that night. Perhaps she was even a little smitten with the handsome Malcolm MacEwan herself.

She chose her white cotton dress with the wide sailor collar trimmed with navy blue piping. And, since it was a special evening, she decided to wear for the first time the white satin dancing slippers her father had sent her from Montreal. Lovingly, she unwrapped her shoes from their protective tissue wrapping. Thoughts of her father turned naturally to thoughts of her parents' marriage. Theirs, too, had been a union of love, one not completely favored by her mother's family. With a sigh that echoed her sadness, she hoped with all her heart that things would work out happily for Abigail and Malcolm.

By the time the King family pulled up at Rose Cottage in their buggy, Sara was dressed and waiting on the porch. Being extra careful not to soil her new white shoes, she minced her way towards the waiting buggy. With a flick of the reins, they set off to dinner at Aunt Abigail's.

And what a dinner it was. The table, stretching the length of the dining room, was overflowing with food. There was the biggest roast of beef Sara had ever laid eyes on, served with golden Yorkshire pudding, green beans, mashed potatoes and plenty of gravy. The room echoed with the clatter of silverware mixed with convivial conversation and merriment.

By now, Abigail's nervousness had abated a

little. She had fretted all day, afraid the party would be a disaster, but everyone was getting on so well. She was so proud of Malcolm. She had been afraid that his manners might not be exactly what they should be, but, to her relief, he had behaved beautifully. He hadn't even spilled a thing the whole dinner. In fact, everyone had been careful. Her best white linen tablecloth was able to survive the whole meal, unmarked.

After dinner, everyone retired to the parlor to tell stories and hear of Malcolm's adventures. In the kitchen, Abigail placed her best china teacups on the tray and carried it to her guests. The sight that greeted her on entering the parlor, made her stop. All her fears and misgivings melted and, for a brief moment, Abigail felt at peace. Surrounded by those she cared about the most sat the man she loved, happily ensconced and holding the full attention of those around him.

"I saw it at a bend in the river, bright and shiny in the moonlight," Malcolm said in a hushed voice.

"Was it gold?" Andrew King asked gravely.

Malcolm paused for a moment. He surveyed the small, eager faces all turned up towards him in anticipation. He winked over at Janet King who sat on the chair opposite.

"No, it was a wee light, beckoning to me. I moved towards it, and I began to see the outline of an old man. But he disappeared, just melted into thin air."

"Was it a ghost?" Felix gulped. He liked to hear stories about ghosts. He shifted around to get more comfortable on the floor. His sister Cecily sat on Mr. MacEwan's lap, her eyes wide with terror.

"Well, I'm not one that believes in such things, but when I told the story in town, they said it must have been Old Man McGinty, telling me where to pan for gold." Malcolm took a satisfied puff of his cigar. Like all good storytellers, he knew the right moment for a pause.

Sara, herself well-skilled in spinning yarns, asked the question she knew he was waiting for.

"Who's Old Man McGinty?"

"A miner from the rush in '97, dead these past five years. They say he was murdered by a jealous partner."

Alec King looked up from his place by the fire. Of all the guests at the party, Alec was the only one who did not seem to be enjoying himself. He did not join in the general conversation, though he would offer the occasional polite smile. The man was an insufferable boor, he thought. Shifting on his stool, he continued to gaze at the flames, lost in his own thoughts.

"Weren't you scared?" Cecily cowered closer to Malcolm for protection.

☙☙☙

Abigail tried to signal Malcolm discreetly with
her eyes, indicating with a spasmodic fluttering
of her lids that he should lower his voice.
But Malcolm, zealously caught up in singing
God's praises, paid her no mind.

❧❧❧❧❧

Sara and Felicity clung for dear life as their aunt
spurred the horse to go faster and faster.

At each turn, at every bump, they were convinced the buggy would fly completely out of control, spilling them fatally onto the road.

❧

"I cannot marry you."
The words struggled out of her tight throat.
"What do you mean, Abby?"
The misery in his question stabbed her, causing her
heart to ache with an echoing pain.

"I'm not afraid of an old ghost story. I went back under the cover of darkness and I put my dish right where he disappeared. And, of course, the rest is history."

"You found gold?" Felix's mouth hung wide open. This was the best story he'd ever heard.

"I did that. And if indeed it was the ghost of Old Man McGinty, I owe him a great debt. He made me my fortune and gave me a chance at happiness." Abigail blushed at his gaze, for she knew what he meant.

Happiness was not a big enough word to encompass the enormity of Malcolm's feelings at that moment. Tonight, he thought, if all goes well, I will have my heart's desire. He stirred a spoonful of sugar into his tea. Removing the spoon, he was just about to lick it dry when a sharp look from Abigail and a quick shake of her head warned him that he was about to commit another one of his social blunders. Hoping no one would notice, he sheepishly placed the spoon down on the saucer. Out of the corner of his eye, he caught Alec King staring at him. Hot shame flooded him up to the roots of his hair.

"Tell us about the grizzly bear again." Felix's request pulled him out of his embarrassment.

"Did it really eat all your supplies?" Sara asked.

"Not just my supplies. It even ate my hat. And it

was my lucky hat, too." He flourished his cigar to add a comic note. The wee bairns are laughing, he thought, and that made him happy.

"Oh, Abigail, do let me give you a hand." Janet rose from her seat and took a tray of dishes from her sister's hands. She seems a little high-strung this evening, Janet thought. Watching her closely, with the concern that is the right of an older sister, Janet followed Abigail into the kitchen where they got started on the washing up.

"I'm delighted that everyone is getting along." Abigail, her smile a bit forced, handed a freshly washed cup to her sister to dry.

"Oh, the children are absolutely smitten with him. Sara and Felicity worship him. And I must say that, despite his change in fortune, he's still the same old Malcolm." Janet hoped that she had said the right thing.

"Though, to be sure, he is very much changed in appearance, isn't he?" Abigail spoke in such a rush, that Janet had no time to reply to the question. "And, I must say, I don't like the mustache, but I haven't the courage to ask him to shave it off. He might be offended."

Janet knew her sister well enough to know that more than the mustache was worrying her. She watched as conflicting emotions struggled on Abigail's face.

"Oh Janet," she blurted out, "I don't know what to do."

All the doubts and fears that had been worrying Abigail over the last few days came out in an unstoppable torrent, "I don't know how to act. And, I must say, I can't help worrying what Father might think. He always said I wasn't the marrying kind."

"Abigail, it suited Father to tell you that. He wanted you to stay at home with him."

"It was nice to be needed, and now it seems that Mr...." she corrected herself, "...Malcolm needs me, too." How could she explain it? She really wasn't sure if she understood it herself. She took a deep breath. "It's just that sometimes, he is so...overwhelming. I'm not used to so much attention. It's exhausting."

"Better that than being ignored." Without meaning to, Janet let slip her own secret pain, her feeling that Alec had lately been ignoring her. *I'm being selfish*, she chastised herself. *Abigail needs me now. It is my sister I should worry about.*

Fortunately, Abigail did not notice Janet's momentary lack of attention. She was too caught up in her own problems.

"Oh, and the presents he gives me. They are positively ugly. The jewellery? Why, I couldn't wear half of it. But...I don't...oh, everything is such a muddle. "I suppose it pleases him to buy me trinkets. I just don't know what to think."

"Oh Abigail, don't think," Janet implored her. "Follow your heart."

"I did that once."

Her bottom lip pouted out and her eyes looked so sad. Poor Abigail, Janet thought. She looked like a child. I do hope she makes the right decision. And for the moment, at least, Janet set aside her own worries to gather her sister in her arms and give her a hug.

Chapter Ten

The party was a great success. Along with the wonderful food and stories, there was music and dancing. The whole evening had that magic quality usually reserved for holidays.

But, as inevitably happens to all good things, the evening finally came to an end. In the hallway, Uncle Alec handed out coats as everyone sleepily said their "thank you's" and "goodbye's."

When it came time for her to take her leave, Sara curtsied.

"Thank you for the lovely party. It's the first time I've actually danced in the satin shoes that Father sent me."

"And magic shoes they must be, Sara, for I've never seen a more graceful lassie." Malcolm gave her a slight bow. His compliment gave her great pleasure, as it praised her father's good taste in clothing and her own dancing abilities.

The night sky winked at them with a thousand eyes. Cecily slept soundly in her father's arms. The rest of the group ambled with a happy weariness towards the buggy.

"Here, let me help get everybody into the wagon," Malcolm offered, bounding off the porch with unfettered enthusiasm.

"No thanks. We can manage." Alec's reply was cold and his manner distant. The chill was wasted on Malcolm. Quick as a wink, he had everyone tucked and bundled warmly into the buggy.

Alec clicked his tongue and shook the reins. The horses obeyed the signal and set off at a leisurely pace back home. Malcolm MacEwan, waving good-bye, was the last thing Sara saw before she drifted off into a deep sleep

Abigail stood warming her hands by the fire. The wavering flames darted and flickered like all the different thoughts that jumped about in her mind.

"Abby." His voice settled her thoughts, but set her heart aflutter. She turned to face him. How handsome he looked to her just now. A warm sensation burst from her heart and suffused her whole being.

"I have something to say to you, and I want to do it proper like." Placing both hands gently on her shoulders, he propelled her towards a chair. It seemed to Abigail that she had floated down into her seat, and if she didn't hold tight, she would fly right up to the ceiling, light as a feather.

Malcolm reached into his pocket and removed a small velvet box. It spoke more eloquently to her than words. He opened it and held it towards her. The large diamond sparkling from its gold band uttered the question burning in Malcolm's mind.

Words left her. She tried to find them, but they had all slipped away. All she could find was a gasp.

"If you'd like a bigger stone, just say the word." Malcolm eyed her anxiously.

"Oh, no, no, it's big enough," she hastily assured him. She had never seen such an enormous diamond in her entire life.

"Do you like it?"

"It's beautiful, Malcolm."

Relief made him bold. It was time to take the next step, the step that would assure his future happiness.

"Abby, I've been practicing to say this for as long as I've known you. Can you find it in your heart to be my wife?"

Abigail averted her eyes, instead looking down at her hands, folded in her lap.

"I don't know, Malcolm," she said softly.

His hopes wavered. Surely she must say yes. Abigail rose from her seat, slowly. Placing her arm on the mantle, she stood gazing into the fireplace. Above her, Malcolm could see the cold eyes of the Reverend Ward glaring down at him. Malcolm waited helplessly, still holding the ring, aching for her answer.

Abigail waited for her thoughts to settle. She could feel her heart pounding in its cage, trying to break free.

"We've been through this before, and you went away. I couldn't bear for that to happen again, not..." She hesitated. "...not after loving you all these years."

"Abby, I love you."

"I want to believe you. I really do. Oh, what will everyone in Avonlea think?"

"The devil what anyone else thinks! Pardon the language." Malcolm quietly beseeched her, "Please say yes."

Their fears and hopes had been spoken. They stood, separated in reality by only a few feet, but divided by seven years of pain and absence. Malcolm stretched his hand across the chasm that estranged them, hoping to heal the rift. Feeling his touch, Abigail quickly withdrew her hand.

"May I not even have your hand to hold, Abby?"

She quickly glanced up to the portrait of her

father. It was he who had denied her happiness. It was he who had turned Malcolm away. But now, through some miracle, she was being given a second chance to have what she realized she had always wanted.

She extended her hand. It trembled slightly as it waited.

"Yes. Yes, Mr. MacEwan."

Tenderly, he grasped her little hand in his. And, with an equal care, he drew her into his embrace, and kissed her.

Chapter Eleven

"He's just showered her with jewellery, apparently. And I couldn't get over the way they acted together, could you?"

She knew her voice sounded silly, but she couldn't stop. Whenever she was nervous or unsure, Janet King talked. She couldn't help it. It was an old habit from childhood. Running off at the mouth is what her father called it. Her mouth was going full speed now, difficult to check.

"It seems a long time since we acted that way...doesn't it?"

But Alec kept to his silence. The children had all been tucked in their beds. The house murmured and rustled as it, too, settled in for the night. Janet blew out one of the lamps in the parlor. The rustle of her starched white cotton nightdress sounded extremely loud in the oppressive stillness. She moved to the next lamp and extinguished it.

Alec, still dressed for dinner, sat brooding by the fire, throwing bits of wood on the flame.

It isn't natural to remain so quiet, she argued to herself. Through fifteen years of marriage, they had always told each other everything. Why the sudden secrecy? Janet hated the estrangement. He was behaving like an ill-mannered boy. She simply had to speak.

"Alec, what is the matter? You certainly weren't very pleasant company this evening. You were almost rude."

"I wasn't rude. I just got sick to death of hearing tales of derring-do, and life in a mining camp, striking it rich and..."

"The man can't help it if he tells an interesting story. And the children were fascinated."

"Mmm-mm." He clamped his mouth shut and turned his attention back to the flames.

Now I've done it, she worried. I jumped in too soon and he's punishing me by refusing to speak.

"I think you might have tried a little bit harder, for Abigail's sake," she chastened.

"Yes, I could have pretended, all right. I'm getting

good at that," he said, with such a note of sadness that it made Janet regret her scolding.

Alec picked up the kerosene lamp from the mantle. He moved heavily, as if he carried the weight of a thousand pounds on each shoulder. He trudged towards the door.

"Are you coming to bed?" she asked timidly.

He stopped. His shoulders hunched as if to protect him from the question. He rested his hand on the latch and he turned his head only partway towards her. "I'd better go check the barn. Chickens got out last night. Felix forgot to put the lock on."

The door opened. Frantically, Janet thought, I can't let him leave like this. She called after him. "Alec?"

He stopped.

"Remember how we used to sleep out there some nights? It's probably a lot more comfortable than that wobbly old bed of ours. I could come with you if you like." She smiled with a shy expectancy.

His eyes winced as if with some pain. His voice caught in his throat. He managed to mumble, "No, you go on up. I'll be in later."

Then he left. Janet stood holding her candle in the darkened room. For what may have been a minute, but seemed like hours, she remained in the cold parlor, confused and feeling so, so lonely.

Chapter Twelve

"Abigail Ward!" Mrs. Lawson extracted herself from behind the counter, glided towards her newly arrived customers and extended a gracious hand. "May I be one of the first to congratulate you on your lovely news." Mrs. Lawson loved weddings. They always made her cry. Why, just the announcement of an engagement alone could make her eyes misty.

She patted Abigail's hand and blinked back the tears of joy that were invading her eyes.

"My goodness. *Look* at that ring. Come see, Mrs. Potts."

"I can see it from here. It looks like a beacon in the night." In Mrs. Potts' mouth, the words sounded more like a criticism than the compliment she no doubt intended them to be.

Abigail looked radiant in her periwinkle-blue suit and her smart new bonnet. She'll make a lovely bride, Mrs. Lawson thought.

Mrs. Lawson took Abigail's hands "Now, I know you're going to need a million things, so don't be afraid to ask if you don't see what you're looking for."

"Well, Janet has convinced me that I need a new dress."

"Dresses," Janet King hastily interjected.

"Then you'll need to look at materials and patterns. Come right this way." Fluttering her hand to indicate that they should follow, Mrs. Lawson flitted across the store, stopping in front of the shelves where the cloth was stored. Materials of all colors and textures were stacked neatly in their cubbyholes. On the bottom ledge lay several pattern books containing the latest styles from New York, Montreal and Paris.

"Oh Abigail, just look at that cream satin for your wedding gown," Janet exclaimed.

"Nonsense, Janet. I'm not a child bride. No, I prefer the mauve taffeta."

"Oh no, don't do that. It's so sombre. If not the cream, then at least the peach."

Lifting both eyebrows by way of encouragement, Mrs. Lawson urged her, "The peach would be lovely on you, with your coloring."

"I'd stick to the mauve taffeta if I were you, Abigail." Mrs. Potts' declaration had its desired effect, putting everyone into a state of confusion.

"My goodness," Mrs. Lawson sputtered, hastily trying to change the subject, "it's going to be so odd calling you Mrs. MacEwan."

"Now that's plain bad luck, Mrs. Lawson, calling someone by their married name before the wedding. Shame on you. Usually ends up the marriage doesn't take place at all. Although, I hope for

your sake, my dear Abigail, that's not the case,"
Mrs. Potts burbled at her with a gooey smile.
"Providence knows it's probably your last chance to
throw off the mantle of maidenhood."

Embarrassment caused everyone, except Mrs.
Potts, to develop a keen interest in something other
than the conversation. Janet indulged a sudden,
overwhelming desire to look through a nearby pattern book, while Mrs. Lawson quickly became
obsessed with a crack she had never before noticed
on the ceiling.

"Oh dear. I don't think that I can decide."
Abigail became so flustered that she almost forgot
why she was in the store at all.

Janet tried, as discreetly as she could, to remind
her.

"Don't forget about your trousseau."

"My what?" Abigail's voice rang clear as a bell
through the fog.

"Your underthings," Janet whispered.

"Oh, Janet, really," Abigail mumbled, her face
turning a shade of red that would make a beet pale
in comparison. With as much aplomb as she could
muster, Abigail turned to Mrs. Lawson.

"I shall have to decide about the material later."

Then, with as much grace and decorum as she
could muster, Abigail bolted from the store.
Clamping her hat securely on her head, Janet thrust

the pattern book upon the unsuspecting Mrs. Lawson and scurried out after her sister.

"You know," Mrs. Lawson opined once the dust had settled and she was alone with Mrs. Potts, "I don't think Abigail Ward has faced the reality of it all."

"It's plain as plain, Mrs. Lawson, that she hasn't."

Both ladies wagged their heads, one in sympathy and one with pity.

Chapter Thirteen

Derek Sutherland mopped his rather florid face with a clean linen handkerchief and prayed that they would all manage to find the right note. As organist and choirmaster of Avonlea, his was an onerous task, but one which he performed dutifully and patiently. The present choir, though zealous, lacked—how could he put it delicately? —a certain musicality. He knew if they could all sing the first note properly, the rest usually followed in due order.

The Reverend Leonard nodded to him to let the hymn commence. Cracking his knuckles, he lifted his hands above the keys and allowed them to waver there for the briefest of moments. The choir watched him expectantly, their mouths half-opened, waiting for the signal to begin. Mr. Sutherland took a deep breath and struck the opening chords of hymn number sixteen. With a great nod of his head, he motioned the choir to join.

Eternal are Thy mercies, Lord

The congregation lifted up their voices in song. The sound blended in a not too unpleasing noise.

Eternal truth attends thy word
Thy praise shall sound from
shore to shore

From the general sea of indistinguishable voices, one leapt forth and made its individuality apparent. Malcolm MacEwan's deep baritone rose up and surged above the rest like a great wave, overpowering all voices around, and nearly drowning out the poor choir, who were helplessly swimming along.

Abigail felt the stab of embarrassment that was becoming all too familiar whenever she was in public with Malcolm. She blushed. She could feel the eyes of the whole congregation burning on her back. She just knew that everybody was looking, though in reality, Mrs. Potts and Mrs. Biggins were the only people who took much notice.

She tried to signal Malcolm discreetly with her eyes, indicating with a spasmodic fluttering of her lids that he should lower his voice. But Malcolm, zealously caught up in singing God's praises, paid her no mind. Abigail was fairly cringing with shame. She prayed that the earth would open up and swallow her whole. Didn't he realize that his behavior reflected badly on her?

Till sun shall rise and set no more

Malcolm lustily belted out the last line, lingering on the final vowel, drawing it out until it could go no further, "Aaa-meeeeeen." Satisfied with his performance, he sat down.

It was with some sorrow, and no little relief, that Abigail settled herself in the pew.

The congregation spilled forth from the white clapboard church into the stillness of a sleepy Avonlea Sunday. Mrs. Potts hurried as quickly as her plump little legs could carry her. She was most anxious to find her friend, Mrs. Biggins, in order to discuss the morning's events. A few people got a sharp elbow in the back as Mrs. Potts pushed her way through the crowd. As self-appointed watchdogs of the community, no one's performance went unnoticed or without comment from these two scrupulous ladies.

At the bottom of the steps, she found Mrs. Biggins. The woeful, slightly superior look her friend greeted her with reflected Mrs. Potts' sentiments exactly. The two gossips linked arms and strolled, each reliving the horror of the morning's event.

"I could almost hear the Reverend Ward roll over in his grave. The man may have money, but he hasn't changed a bit in other respects." Mrs. Potts raised her voice a notch in order to let her opinion be more generally heard. "He's still a philistine," she hissed. "Can you imagine—singing at the top of his lungs like that?"

Of course, neither of the good ladies could imagine such a thing for themselves, or any other God-fearing person for that matter.

As they approached Reverend Leonard, Mrs. Potts increased the volume of her discourse even more, in order to include the minister in her confidence. She hoped to find in the good Reverend an ally.

"Why, he completely drowned out the choir."

"And for that," Reverend Leonard placed his hands together as if in prayer and rolled his eyes heavenward, "may we be truly thankful." Then he smiled indulgently on his faithful, but somewhat misguided, parishioners.

Mrs. Potts toddled off in a huff, dragging with her the equally piqued Mrs. Biggins. "It will never work, you mark my words," she announced prophetically. To that, Mrs. Biggins could only agree.

Abigail left the church arm in arm with Malcolm.

She completely expected, as she exited the building, to be met with a host of sniggers and derisive stares. Instead, the couple was greeted with only the heartiest of congratulations and the most sincere wishes for happiness. Her chagrin lessened as she realized that perhaps she was being foolish to think that everyone had judged Malcolm so severely. She was almost totally at ease until she looked around and glimpsed the harsh countenances of Mrs. Potts and Mrs. Biggins glaring in her direction.

Her cheeks burned crimson.

"Oh Abigail, dear, you do look radiant." Janet King mistook the the high color on Abigail's cheeks for a sign of happiness. "Have you decided on a date yet? Felicity will give me absolutely no rest about a new dress." Janet took Abigail's hands and gently drew her away to a more quiet spot, in the hope that she might be able to urge her to decide on a date for the wedding. That Abigail had not yet named the day was making everyone uneasy.

With Janet and Abigail off by themselves, Malcolm MacEwan and Alec King were suddenly left facing each other. They had nothing to say. So, to avoid great social discomfort, they took the normal course offered in such an eventuality. They smiled at one another. The relief was momentary, and they were soon left with a disquieting pause between them. So, to ease the situation, they smiled again.

Malcolm was rarely at a loss for words. Alec King was the only man who could tie his tongue. As a boy, Malcolm had envied, almost worshipped, the accomplished and wealthy Alec. He longed to be his friend, but the more popular, slightly older Alec shunned his companionship. It was not contempt that made Alec so callous, it was just the usual thoughtlessness that accompanies boyhood. Even though he was now rich, the impoverished boy in Malcolm still felt a little out of place next to the privileged offspring of the influential King family.

Fortunately, Malcolm and Alec were rescued from a potentially disastrous situation by the arrival of Mr. Lawson. Twinkling with the knowledge that he held important information, Mr. Lawson scampered over and positioned himself between the two men. After hastily greeting Alec, he turned his attention to the man whose respect and patronage he wanted to earn.

"Mr. MacEwan, just wanted to let you know, since you asked me about properties in the area. There's a big auction in Carmody on Wednesday." He paused and adjusted his glasses with a wrinkling of his nose. "House and contents."

"You mean Raffe Johnson's homestead?" Alec asked.

"That's the one." Mr. Lawson nodded. "I'd go myself..." Lawson's voice lowered and thickened with candor, "but the wife and I don't see eye to eye on auctions. Anyway, just thought I'd let you know." Then he smiled the self-satisfied smirk of one who knows that he has just delivered meaningful news.

"And I'm truly grateful, Mr. Lawson." Malcolm stared pointedly at Alec. "I can never resist the thrill of a good bidding match."

"Edward!" Mrs. Lawson brayed from her carriage.

"Excuse me," Mr. Lawson said, humbly taking his leave.

"I might have a look around there myself," Alec said casually. The challenge in Malcolm MacEwan's last statement had not gone unnoticed by him.

With a hardy whack that was meant to be friendly, Malcolm slapped Alec on the back. Joking, he warned, "Ah, there won't be room for the two of us, Alec King. Now, where did those women go?"

Alec King glared, not exactly kindly, at the back of the departing Malcolm MacEwan.

Chapter Fourteen

Felix was happier than a pig in mud. It wasn't every day that he got to go to Carmody. And it wasn't every day that he went to an auction, either. Come to think of it, he couldn't recollect ever having gone to an auction. That made today all the more special.

Felix gloated on that for a while. He had already exhausted the thrill of being able to go while the girls had to stay home. That thought had occupied him for at least three miles before he'd got tired of it.

Might as well gloat, because there was no one to talk to. His father was keeping pretty silent. He'd answer if Felix asked him a question, but most of the time he just drove and stared straight ahead. Every once in a while he'd whistle, never a whole song, just snatches of it.

Both his parents had been pretty quiet lately. It looked like they weren't speaking much to each other. Felix reckoned someone had done something wrong. He didn't know which one, but he was sure glad it wasn't him for a change.

The auction was in full swing by the time Alec drove the buggy through the gates of the Johnson farm and parked it in the shade of one of the large maple trees that lined the drive.

Crowds of people milled around the yard in the warm autumn sunlight. All over the lawn were tables piled high with the effects of the Johnson family: books, lamps, a china tea set painted with red roses, glass vases of various shapes and colors, several ornate silver picture frames—all the objects that make up a family's history.

Alec meandered around the tables, casually examining the items. The stuff didn't interest Felix much. The only table he wanted to see was the one across the yard that had lemonade, cookies and cakes for sale. He pulled on his father's arm to get his attention, but Alec just shook him off. He obviously wasn't as hungry as Felix.

In front of the large, gray farmhouse was a platform made just for the occasion. Felix figured the roly-poly man wearing the bowler hat must be the auctioneer. He stood on the platform and talked a mile a minute, pointing here, pointing there, with a wooden hammer held in his hand. Then, all of a sudden, BANG, he smacked the hammer down on the wooden crate in front of him. Felix nearly jumped out of his skin, he was so surprised.

"Sold to the gentleman with the mustache in the first row," the auctioneer bawled, pointing with his gavel.

Malcolm MacEwan beamed with pride as he received the amethyst necklace and earring set from the auctioneer's assistant. Malcolm pictured to himself how happy Abby would be when she saw the gift, when she saw all the gifts he was going to give her. He chuckled inwardly and took a big satisfied puff on his cigar.

"That was the last item of jewellery and silverware," drawled the assistant, a scrawny man with a prominent Adam's apple that bobbed up and down as he spoke. "We'll now be moving on to the kitchen and bedroom furnishings."

The auctioneer leaned towards Malcolm and asked, with mock earnestness, "Would you be interested in a buggy, sir, to cart everything home in?" His black eyes twinkling in his round, fleshy face were the only indication that he was having Malcolm on.

"No, sir," Malcolm replied. "It's all to stay put. For I'm to buy the house, too."

The people around laughed good-naturedly at his bravado. Some clapped in approval. Malcolm saluted them with a bow of his head and his uplifted cigar.

The assistant and his boy staggered under the weight of the next item on the list. Struggling, they placed a beautiful, solid-oak bedframe on the block. It was a stately piece of furniture. The high headboard scrolled back and on the footboard were carved three stylized flowers. The wood itself was polished a rich, reddish brown. From his position in the yard, Alec admired it.

"Look, Felix. Do you think your mother would like a bed like that? That rickety one at home's not worth fixing."

Felix considered the piece of furniture in question.

"I don't know, Pa. The back's too big. You couldn't hang your shirt on it."

Alec chuckled and pulled the brim of Felix's hat down over his eyes. "Well, she's always hankered for a bed like that. I think she could use a present."

"Hey, yeah," Felix suggested as he pulled his cap back into place, "maybe she'll start speaking to you again."

His father didn't take his suggestion too kindly. With a stiff motion of his mouth, something between a smile and a grimace of pain, Alec took Felix firmly by the arm and led him to the circle of bidders.

"Ten, am I bid ten. Ten dollars," the auctioneer asked expectantly.

"Ten dollars," shouted a man in a dark, gray suit.

"Ten-dollar bid. Now ten and a half. Ten and a half," the auctioneer yodeled.

"Eleven," came a voice from the crowd.

"Eleven, now a bid of twelve? Twelve?"

"Twelve," Malcolm called.

Felix recognized Malcolm MacEwan's voice. He craned his neck, searching through the crowd until he found him. Felix raised his arm to wave to Mr. MacEwan, but his father quickly stopped him before he accidentally bid. Malcolm turned and saw Alec and Felix. Nodding his head in their direction, he smiled. Felix, pleased with the gesture, grinned back.

"Twelve-dollar bid. Now a bid of thirteen?" The auctioneer waved his gavel around like a pointer.

"Thirteen," bid the man in the gray suit.

"Thirteen. Got a bid now. Fourteen. Now bidding fifteen dollars."

"Fifteen," shouted Alec King. Felix stared at his father in amazement. The whole thing was getting exciting now.

"Sixteen," countered Malcolm MacEwan.

The auctioneer swung his gavel in Malcolm's direction. "Sixteen, got a bid. Then seventeen..."

"Seventeen," roared a man in a derby hat.

"Eighteen," countered the man in the gray suit.

"Eighteen, we're at seventeen now and eighteen," sang the auctioneer.

"Twenty," Alec bid.

"*Twenty*-dollar bid here. Now twenty-one?"

"Twenty-three," roared the derby hat.

"Twenty-five," Malcolm hollered, raising his cigar.

"Twenty-five dollars." The auctioneer urged them on with his voice. "Got a bid now on twenty-six. Do I hear twenty-six?"

Alec could feel his anger rising. Malcolm MacEwan was deliberately raising the bidding. Refusing to be outdone, he shouted, "Thirty!"

"Thirty-dollar bid over here.... Now thirty-one."

Felix grew concerned. "Pa, you don't need it that badly."

Alec wasn't listening. His eyes were set in a stubborn gaze. His fists were clenched and his lips were clamped tight.

"That's thirty, one thirty-dollar bid here. And one, one, you want to go one?" the auctioneer goaded. "It's your turn, sir, for thirty-one dollars...?"

"That's a lot of money, Pa."

"Thirty-one? One thirty-dollar bid here, going, going..."

"Fifty dollars," Malcolm bellowed.

Malcolm's bid was like a slap in the face. Alec knew he couldn't compete with that kind of money, and he knew MacEwan knew it too. He felt he had been played for a fool, toyed with like a mouse by a malicious cat. Well, Alec King wouldn't be treated that way.

"Fifty-dollar bid, now. Bid him at fifty. Bid him a one? One? Fifty dollars, going...going...gone!" The auctioneer slammed down the gavel. The sound of it rocked Alec to the pit of his stomach.

Malcolm MacEwan turned and saluted him. Alec narrowed his eyes and scowled in return. Grabbing the unwitting Felix by the arm, he turned on his heels and stomped through the crowd. Poor Felix was hard-pressed to keep up.

Malcolm caught up to them at the buggy. Felix was already up, and Alec had just unhitched the horses and was about to climb up himself when he was accosted by the one person in the whole world he was not happy to see.

"Alec, no hard feelings. Just a little healthy

competition, that's all, just like the old days." Malcolm tried to cajole Alec, but both men knew it wasn't like the old days at all. In the old days, Malcolm had always lost.

"I must say, it's refreshing that we meet on more equal terms." Malcolm smiled and extended his hand. He was willing to let bygones be bygones.

His words had the effect of salt in an open sore.

"We wouldn't be on equal terms, MacEwan," Alec spat, "if you had all the money in Christendom."

Alec climbed on the buggy and pulled off in a fury. Malcolm MacEwan was left alone in the settling dust.

Chapter Fifteen

The whole thing was a disaster, an unmitigated disaster. There was no other way to describe it. Tears burned her eyes, and, too tired to fight, she let them trickle down her cheeks. Abigail knew she would have to make a choice. She most definitely couldn't go on this way.

Her knees ached. It was the fourth time in two days that she had been forced to scrub her parlor floor. She sat back on her heels. Her hair was falling out of its bun and hung limply around her face, as if it, too, were too weary to tidy itself up.

I ask him to wipe his boots, but he doesn't listen, Abigail complained silently to an invisible and, she hoped, sympathetic listener. She took one final swipe at the floor, then tossed the cloth disdainfully into the pail. Insolent droplets of dirty water leapt from the bucket and splattered on the freshly clean floor, as if to mock her efforts. Poor Abigail was too fatigued to be provoked.

Rising from her knees with no little discomfort, she picked up the bucket. All around her were vases filled with flowers, tokens of Malcolm's love for her. She knew he loved her, and that made her glad. Sometimes, though, she wished he wouldn't love her so much. Or was it that he loved her the wrong way?

Marriage was a matter of compromise, she knew that, but it seemed that all the negotiations so far had been one-sided. It's true, she reminded herself, he has amended his manners and bought new clothes, but that was only as it should be in genteel society. It's just...

Abigail didn't quite know just what it was. All she knew was that the house was always a mess. She didn't appreciate spending her days cleaning up after someone who had no respect for a well-scrubbed house. Cleanliness was important to her, and he was going to have to learn to respect it.

Her resolution added a certain determination to

her step, but the sight that confronted her in the kitchen caused her spirits to flag. Dishes smeared with half-eaten food lay casually on the table. Cigar ash was sprinkled liberally, anointing the food and whatever else struck its fancy. Chairs were scattered higgledy-piggledy, dislodged from their proper places. And the greatest insult—muddy bootprints tracked from the door to the table as clear as a diagram in a ballroom dancing book.

Abigail's heart sank. The confusion overwhelmed her, threatening to destroy the carefully ordered life she had so diligently built as a protection for herself. She hated chaos. She had fought all her life to keep it away. Now, it looked as if it were going to break down the fortress she had erected and sweep her away. Abigail was frightened. The diamond ring weighed heavily on her finger, carrying the whole weight of her indecision.

Malcolm MacEwan was as proud as a chap could be as he drove his buggy through Avonlea. He had been a poor boy when he'd lived here last, but now he was a rich man. The springs of his carriage sang with the weight of their load. The bed he had outbid Alec for—fair and square, mind you— rode proudly aloft in the buggy, a symbol of his love for his intended bride.

Mrs. Potts' eyes nearly popped from her face,

and it looked like Mrs. Biggins might swoon. Had he no shame, carting around such a personal item of furniture as though it were nothing more than a kitchen table? Malcolm chuckled and saluted them handsomely as he passed. The big-hearted Malcolm had no time for small-minded people.

"Morning, Reverend. Thanks for the tip on the auction, Mr. Lawson," Malcolm called as he passed in front of the general store. Mr. Lawson feebly returned his greeting, lifting his hand tentatively in the air as if to say, "You're welcome...I think."

Malcolm couldn't wait to see Abby's surprise. Wouldn't she be tickled when she heard the news. He was bursting with excitement himself. A grand house, big enough for the two of them and several children to boot. That was a gift to be proud of. For years he had dreamed of showering Abby with presents. It was the least he could do to repay her for the kindness of loving him. His dream had finally come true.

With a final sweep of the duster, order had at last been restored. Abigail's thoughts regained a certain equanimity once the house had been coerced back to cleanliness. She would have a talk with him, and he would just have to listen to her. If he didn't, well, she would be forced to take steps. What steps, she hadn't quite worked out yet.

A thunderous pounding on the door rattled her resolve. Who could it be but Malcolm? Screwing up her courage, she went to answer it. She was saved from the trouble, however, when Malcolm barrelled in, unbidden, and pounced upon his bride-to-be.

"Malcolm, did you use the scraper outside?" she asked firmly, once she had recovered.

"Nope," he bragged, childishly pleased with his transgression.

"Your feet are covered in mud. I just washed the floor!"

"Don't fuss so, Abby," Malcolm replied lightly, dismissing her concerns.

"Ooh, Malcolm!" Abigail stamped her foot in frustration. With a deep breath, she calmed herself. Remembering her decision, she launched bravely into her topic.

"Please sit down. We must have a discussion about the state you leave this house in."

Malcolm had other ideas. He swept her into his arms as if both her person and her request had little weight.

"But I have something to say to you, my darlin'."

"Malcolm, no. Put me down. Put me down!" she screamed, kicking and flailing. "Put me down right now!" How dare he use his size against her. "Stop it!! Put me down!!!!"

Malcolm did not heed her request. He knew she

wasn't really mad. He figured she'd settle down once she saw what he'd brought her.

After carrying her out the door, down the porch steps and along the path, Malcolm finally put her down by the picket fence. Beaming with pride, he waved his hand towards his gift.

"It's my wedding present to you. Well, what do you think?"

Abigail was not capable of saying what was going on in her mind at that moment. The sight of a bed sitting blatantly in front of her house momentarily suspended her ability to speak. A mad fury rose up inside of her, but she held it back.

Malcolm was oblivious to her mood.

"The moment I saw it, I knew it was the sort of thing a lady like you should have. It'll look fine in our new house."

At first, Abigail wasn't sure if she had heard correctly. As the words filtered through, the meaning of his statement became all too clear.

"What new house?"

"In Carmody. I bought it at the auction not an hour ago. I wish you could have seen it, there was nobody could outbid me. And you'd have laughed to see the people gawking at this bed as I drove through Avonlea." Malcolm chuckled with the memory.

Abigail was mortified. "You drove that bed

through Avonlea?" Each word dropped like a brick. The nerve of the man, flaunting their privacy in town.

The thin thread of her resolve snapped. The raging fury she had tried to keep back unleashed itself. She shook her fists in frustration, stamped her foot and then turned and stormed into the house without scraping her feet. She slammed the door so hard the windows rattled.

This was not the reaction Malcolm had anticipated.

Chapter Sixteen

The flowers sat innocently in their vases, sweet declarations of love. They irked her. Venting her rage, Abigail ripped the tender blooms from their pots and hurled them into the fireplace.

"I hope I've done nothing to offend you, Abby." Malcolm stood helplessly in the doorway. "But we *are* engaged." He was surprised by her actions, but, he had to admit, he loved her zest. Mistaking her wrath for high spirits, he coddled her. "Sit yourself down. We need to talk things out." He placed the cigar back in his mouth and extended his hands gently towards her in an effort to guide her to a waiting chair.

With a deliberate jerk of her shoulders, she

shook him off. "If we talk at all," her ire added force
to her words, "it will be about the house that you
have apparently bought in Carmody. And how dare
you disgrace me like that, parading a bed through
the streets of Avonlea? Why, I'll never be able to
hold my head up in the village again!"

Slowly, Malcolm removed the cigar from his
mouth and unthinkingly tapped it. The ash freed
itself and scattered on the oriental carpet. Grabbing
her handkerchief, Abigail scooped down and gath-
ered the offending dust.

Malcolm couldn't understand why she would
do such a thing at an important time like this. He
chided her gently.

"Oh, don't worry about that. I don't mind a litter."

"Well I do. I am constantly cleaning up after you."

"I'll give you a hand, then. I won't let you do it
by yourself."

"I'm used to doing things by myself, Mr.
MacEwan," she shouted, and even she was taken
aback by the strength of her words.

They both stood there shaking, one from anger,
the other from fear and confusion. Poor Malcolm
could not fathom why she was making such a fuss.
He attributed it to the female disposition which, he
had always assumed, was more finely strung than a
man's. He had better be gentle.

"Oh, you're just a wee bit nervous, Abby. It's

time we settled on a date. Come on," he urged her, "name the day."

"*Don't*, Mr. MacEwan."

"Malcolm."

The steps she must take were clear to her now. It was if a bright light shone to lead her along the path of her decision. She steeled herself against the onerous task.

"There is something I must say to you."

She didn't know how she was able to make her legs move, but she did. She settled herself into a chair. She saw his expression, one of pain and bewilderment. Burdened by a weight that was heavy on his heart, Malcolm dropped into a chair.

"I cannot marry you." The words struggled out of her tight throat.

"What do you mean, Abby?"

The misery in his question stabbed her, causing her heart to ache with an echoing pain. She took a deep breath and continued along the way she knew she must go.

"I cannot marry you," she repeated, this time with more conviction.

"What?" The word was only a whisper.

The whole explanation flooded out at once.

"I knew you wouldn't understand. You don't realize what it's like for a woman to give up everything she has—her own house, her own friends, all her past—and move to a place that's far away."

His head was reeling so that he couldn't decide whether she was crazy or he was. It didn't make sense.

"But Carmody isn't very far away," he attempted to reason.

"Well, it might as well be on the other side of the moon as far as I'm concerned. I don't know a living soul there."

"Why didn't you say so before I bought the place, then?" he demanded angrily.

"Because you never asked me, Mr. MacEwan!" She shouted so loudly, she scared herself.

In his agitation, Malcolm vaulted from his chair and paced around the room like a pent-up tiger. Desperately, he tried to appease her.

"But it's not too late. I can sell it and buy right here in Avonlea, if that will please you. But there isn't half as nice a place to be had," he argued, stubbornly missing the point.

"No. Please, Malcolm. That doesn't solve the problem. Oh, I just knew that you wouldn't understand." She didn't know how to explain it to him sensitively without hurting his feelings. She decided to take the blame on herself.

"My ways are not your ways, and I cannot make them over. You track mud into the house, and you don't mind it when things aren't tidy."

Malcolm stopped short. "What the devil, Abby? You must be joking." He couldn't believe what he was hearing. Her little jest cut him to the bone. "I might be a bit careless—a mining camp isn't a place to learn finicky ways—but you can teach me. You're not going to throw me over because I don't wipe my boots?"

She was shaking so badly she couldn't sit still. Rising up, she walked to the fireplace. She could feel her resolve slipping. Gripping the mantlepiece for support, she repeated her vow and took comfort in the very repetition.

"I cannot marry you."

Malcolm pleaded desperately.

"Abby, you can't mean it. I'll do anything. I'll go anywhere. I'll be anything you want, only don't go back on me like this. You're breaking my heart." His voice cracked in his throat.

"I cannot marry you." She turned and faced him. "That is my final word."

"Abby—"

Her path was chosen, there was no turning back. She twisted the diamond ring off her finger and held it out to him.

His whole world exploded. He felt hollow and insubstantial, the way one feels in a dream. Surely, he would wake up soon and rejoice in the knowledge that it was nothing more than the vain wanderings of his mind. But no, this was no fancy, he realized with a cold, sinking feeling.

The diamond flashed, mocking his once bright hopes. Malcolm waved his hand in annoyance, as if to ward off its brilliance. His words were quiet and firm.

"Please, don't do that. I may not have the manners you want, but I have my pride."

As if to demonstrate that very fact, he strode out and slammed the door on his last chance for happiness.

Her breath came quickly. The relief she had hoped for didn't arrive. It hadn't been pleasant, but Abigail had done what she knew she must. *Life wasn't always easy, wasn't that right?* her eyes wordlessly asked the portrait of her father. The Reverend Ward glared down his response.

With no slight trepidation, Abigail wondered what on earth she had just done.

Chapter Seventeen

The news that the marriage of Abigail Ward to Malcolm MacEwan was off caused some concern to the inhabitants of Avonlea. Most were saddened, for they all liked the couple and wished them no harm. The only person who received any satisfaction from the tidings was Mrs. Potts, and that was only because it always gave her great pleasure to say, "I told you so."

Sara and Felicity were heartbroken, as much for their own sakes as for Malcolm and Abigail. They both had been looking forward to the wedding with such great anticipation that they were filled with dismay when they heard it was not to take place.

As soon as the girls learned of the disappointed plans, they rushed over to offer solace to Abigail, who, they were convinced, must be suffering greatly. Sara had visions of her wasting away with sorrow. Her usually reddish complexion would be pale with grief, her eyes red and swollen from an excess of tears. She would be thin, and so weak from anguish that she would be forced to recline all day on the couch.

Sara pictured her there, supine, one hand dangling towards the floor clutching a wet and much crumpled hankie, while the other hand lay, palm up, on her brow. Copious tears would well up in her eyes and pour, unchecked, down her cheeks. Of course, as Felicity pointed out, tears naturally flow into your ears when you are lying on your back, not, as Sara would have it, down your cheeks. But Sara dismissed such scientific detail, claiming instead poetic licence. Cheeks sounded far more romantic than ears.

With such a dire picture in mind, they rushed through the gate, up to the porch, scraped their feet and knocked at Abigail's door. They were much surprised to find their aunt healthy, quite chipper, and going about her tasks as if nothing had happened.

Sara felt something false in all that good show. She sensed that Abigail's stilted smile and overly cheery voice concealed a great pain inside.

When she'd first met Abigail, she had to admit, she had not immediately been taken with her. She'd found her stiff and fussy, a bit comical, perhaps. Then Malcolm MacEwan had come into her life. Love had softened her rigidity and happiness opened her heart.

Now it seemed she had thrown it all away and reverted to her old, obdurate self. Sara couldn't understand why, and desperately wanted to ask Abigail why she'd told Malcolm to leave. There was something in this story that just didn't make sense.

The girls hadn't seen Malcolm since the engagement had been broken, but Sara had overheard Mrs. Biggins telling the Lawsons that he was a broken man. She shivered at the image such words brought to mind.

There was no doubt about it. Sara and Felicity simultaneously concurred that it was up to them to contrive some way to reunite Malcolm and Abigail. It was agreed that Sara would ask Aunt Hetty if she could spend the night at the King farm, so that she and Felicity could talk together.

Only after much pleading, and after Sara had informed her that it was a matter of life and death, did Aunt Hetty agree. As Hetty was not one, she assured Sara, who wished to meddle in the workings of either Creation or corruption, she relented and let Sara stay over at her cousin's.

Well after they had been sent to bed, the girls still deliberated, sitting huddled under the multicolored quilt. The light from their candle surrounded them with a yellow glow, creating for them a bright island in a sea of darkness. They discussed the situation over and over, wondering what they could do.

Janet King sat at the old kitchen table darning an interminable pile of socks. The washing boiled away in a pot on the stove. Her husband sat across from her, reading his newspaper.

There was still an uneasiness between them. It was nothing Janet could exactly put her finger on, but something was wrong. She was afraid to speak to Alec about it, maybe it was all in her imagination. He acted in a pleasant enough manner, she supposed, and, for the most part, his behavior with the children was as it always had been. But with her, Alec had been withdrawn, secretive. It was as if he were only half there.

"Who would have expected it? They seemed so happy." Janet knew that if she talked, Alec would be forced to respond. "Abigail, of course, is completely back to normal. At least that's the way it seems."

Alec looked up from his paper and peered at her over his glasses. "I knew the minute she really got to know MacEwan she wouldn't be able to see it through."

"I'm going to miss Malcolm," Janet mused fondly. "I've heard he sold the farm near Carmody, with all the contents, to one of the other bidders. He lost money, of course. It's all the talk in town today."

"At least there's some justice in the world," Alec grumbled.

Upstairs, plans were not progressing. After more than an hour of intensive thought, Sara and Felicity had reached no conclusions as to how they could best effect the reunion of Malcolm and Abigail. They both decided that a cup of warm milk might aid them in their thinking. Donning their slippers, they tiptoed down the back stairs towards the kitchen.

The sound of her parents' voices made Felicity signal Sara to halt. From the tone of their voices, the girls could tell something was amiss. Crouching together in their white cotton nighties, they listened.

"You seem a little too pleased with someone else's misfortune. That's a wonderful attitude, I must say." Janet put down her darning and looked at her husband.

"Attitude? I don't have any attitude," Alec assured her with a smirk.

"Oh yes you do, Alec King." Janet was furious now. She had put up with his smugness for long enough. Rising angrily from her chair, she went over to the laundry boiling on the stove and poked it mercilessly with a long wooden spoon, as if it were the one to blame. Then she put down the spoon and faced the real culprit. "What in heaven's name is the matter with you? Ever since that man came to town, you've been nearly impossible to live with."

"Nonsense. Why should that man have any effect on me whatsoever?"

"It's beyond me. But you do have a bee in your bonnet, and I wish to high heavens you'd let it out."

Alec removed his glasses and slowly stood up. He regarded her closely.

"Oh, so now I don't even have the freedom of my own thoughts. Even those are to be curtailed."

"Don't be ridiculous. You've all the freedom in the world."

"Look at me, Janet." He spoke with such vehemence that it gave her a start. "I'm forty-three years old, and I've never really lived my life."

She was flabbergasted. "What are you talking about? You were forty-four last birthday."

"Thank you," Alec answered, the words heavy with sarcasm.

"Anyway, Alec..." Janet tried to lighten the situation. If it were only his age he was worried about, she could console him. "...what does it matter?"

"What have I got to show for it?"

"You've got your family. You've got the respect of everyone who knows you. You've got the farm. What more could you ask for?" This was all very confusing to her. She couldn't understand what he was talking about at all.

"The farm was my father's. All I did was stay on it."

"Somebody had to take over the farm. You made a responsible choice."

The words goaded him. "All I've ever made are responsible choices. I've never taken chances or been adventurous. I've never traveled any farther away than Halifax, because husbands don't *do* that. Fathers don't *do* that. They're responsible."

"Oh, well, I'm *terribly* sorry if you think I've stood in your way, if I've kept you from living your life." His words pained her so, she could only respond with anger. "I thought we had a good life."

"It's not that, Janet," he tried to explain. "I just wish that I could have made something of myself, *by* myself. I could have gone to university. I didn't. I could have left the Island, seen more of the world. I didn't. Look at MacEwan. He goes away a beggar, he comes back a hero."

"You're jealous, Alec King!" Janet gloated to hide the pain his words caused her. "Nothing more than that. You're jealous of Malcolm MacEwan."

She turned furiously towards the stairs, hoping with her departure to demonstrate just how she felt. But there was more to be said, and she was going to say it. Turning back abruptly, she faced her husband.

"Well, if you're so dissatisfied with your life, maybe you ought to go with him," she hurled at him, her voice filled with tears and anger.

Sara and Felicity had just enough time to make it up the stairs before Janet came running up. They watched with trepidation as Janet, tears streaming down her face, raced to her bedroom and slammed the door.

Chapter Eighteen

The sun on his face woke him. Alec opened his eyes and blinked at the brightness. Down below, a horse whinnied, then snorted.

Alec stretched, breathing in the sweetness of the hay. Every bone in his body ached. Several of his joints creaked, voicing their complaints about the night's accommodations.

He hadn't slept well in the barn. He had tossed and turned most of the night. His thoughts gave him no rest. Alec regretted what he had said, all the selfish things he had been thinking these past weeks. Now that his fears were out in the open, they seemed a bit foolish to him.

Alec rose up and pulled some hay from his hair. He wondered what time it might be as he walked towards the loft window. The chickens were probably as mad at him now as Janet was. They hated when he was late with their breakfast.

In the fresh morning light, the farm looked strange to him. It was as if he were seeing it for the first time.

From down below came a clattering. Alec peered out but could not see the source of the noise. Climbing down from the loft, he made his way through the cool darkness of the barn out into the stark brightness of the morning.

Malcolm MacEwan was untying the ropes that anchored the solid-oak bedframe to his buggy. He would have cut a handsome figure in his traveling clothes if his face had not appeared so haggard and pale.

"Malcolm." Alec was genuinely surprised to see him. "What can I do for you?"

"Alec." Malcolm smiled a bit sheepishly. He turned his eyes away from the man and kept them intent upon the knots. "I couldn't leave town without apologizing for the way I behaved at the auction. I get a kick out of bidding and, well, I never know when to stop. It's nothing personal." The last knot came undone and the rope slipped free.

Alec flushed with embarrassment at the memory of his own behavior at the auction. He was not proud of the way he had acted.

"No harm done. Got a bit carried away myself." Alec leaned one arm on the buggy. For a moment, neither man spoke.

It was Alec who finally broke the silence.

"What are you doing with the bed?"

"Well, you bid on it fair and square. I thought I'd leave it for you."

"Don't be ridiculous. It's yours."

A spasm of pain momentarily twisted Malcolm's features. "I have no use for it." Sorrow lent a weariness to his words.

"I don't have much use for it either," Alec replied, his voice hoarse with bitterness.

"You could have fooled me, man, the way you were bidding on it."

"I thought Janet might like it." Alec turned his face towards Malcolm and looked him straight in the eye. He wanted to be honest to make up for his harsh words at the auction, words he was now so deeply ashamed of. "The only reason I bid so high was because you did."

Malcolm met his gaze. "I guess the two of us made a fortune for that auctioneer."

"We made Raffe Johnson a very happy man."

The two men smiled at their folly. Whatever awkwardness had been between them melted, and was gone forever.

"Please keep it," Malcolm entreated.

"All right, if it's no use to you. But let me pay you for it."

"No, if there's one thing I don't need, it's more money. It hasn't done me a bit of good so far." The hollow grief that had been his constant companion for the last week was in his voice.

The two men lifted the frame from the buggy and placed it heavily on the ground. Alec straightened up and wiped his hands on his shirt. He was surprised to see how broken and miserable MacEwan looked. Alec felt he should offer some comfort, but the best he could do was polite conversation.

"So, uh, I hear you're leaving the Island."

"I'm going back to the Yukon, where I belong. There's no reason for me to stay. But, in a way, it's put my soul to rest, knowing that she's refused me for herself this time, not because her father said so."

Night after night and all day long, Malcolm had gone over the reasons a thousand times. He knew he was to blame. Now he needed to talk, and he addressed the one man whose opinion he respected.

"I know what you've been thinking these past few weeks, Alec. And you're right. I was never good enough for her."

"I never said that." Alec was stunned, and then ashamed. He realized even more clearly how terribly he had acted.

"She deserves better," Malcolm insisted.

"She might change her mind."

"No." Malcolm had accepted the inevitable. He was too old to cling to unrealistic hopes. "You'll keep an eye on her for me, will you?" he quietly requested. Alec nodded sincerely, with regret that he had not made an effort to know this man better.

Malcolm climbed up on his buggy. Alec stood beside him and extended his hand. Malcolm grasped it and held it for a moment, and smiled down at Alec.

"As a boy, I used to imagine what it would be like living on this farm. It's a piece of land I've always admired. I was really rather envious of you," Malcolm confessed. "I suppose I still am."

Alec laughed out loud at the irony. He was just about to admit that he had envied Malcolm's adventures when he was interrupted by two piercing yells of recognition.

Sara and Felicity came barreling around the corner of the barn and greeted Alec as if he had been away for years. Panting and huffing, Felicity clung to his coat.

"Father, there you are. Mother's been looking all over for you."

Alec gave Felicity's head a gentle pat. He smiled over at his niece, who was regarding him with a look of such great concern that he knew then, as he had known all along, that he would not trade the love of his family for all the gold or all the adventures in the world.

Malcolm MacEwan observed the scene with a bemused envy. What dear lasses, he thought to himself.

Felicity saw him and remembered her manners.

"Hello, Mr. MacEwan."

"Hello young ladies." He tipped his hat. "Well, I had best be going. I have to catch the coach at two o'clock."

"The coach?" Sara asked with a rising dismay.

"To the train station. I'm leaving the Island for the wilds, Sara. There's a grizzly bear that owes me a hat." Malcolm winked at her. "The best of luck to you, Alec, and to Janet and your wonderful family. You're a lucky man."

Looking around at the land he loved so much, Malcolm MacEwan drove away. He knew in his heart he would never see it again.

Chapter Nineteen

Abigail Ward sat in her spotless parlor knitting a throw. She hummed a little tune to keep herself company. Things had all worked out for the best, she told herself. She had put her thoughts through so many twists and loops over the past few days in order to justify what she had done that her thinking had become completely knotted. In all that jumble, she had convinced herself that she was content.

A sudden pounding at the door made her heart flutter. In spite of herself, she was pleased. She knew Malcolm would come to see her eventually. She smoothed her hair.

"Aunt Abigail?" Felicity called from the hallway.

Abigail quelled her disappointment. With a cheery voice she inquired, "Did you wipe your feet? How many times do I have to tell you?"

But the situation was too urgent for the finer points of cleanliness. Sara and Felicity came tearing into the parlor. From the moment they'd heard Malcolm's news, they knew they must act and act quickly. They'd run all the way from the King farm to Abigail's house, not stopping even once.

Abigail started at the sight of her two nieces. Their faces were flushed from running and their expressions were wild.

"Aunt Abigail," Sara managed to pant out, "Malcolm MacEwan is leaving. He's going back to the Yukon. He's catching the two o'clock coach to the station this very afternoon."

Abigail was thunderstruck. "Leaving? Why, you must be mistaken."

"But why?" Sara leveled an accusing eye. "Didn't you tell him to leave?"

"Well, but I never expected him to!" Abigail dropped down in her chair. Panic seized her. "Oh Lord, what am I going to do? Oh, Felicity, Sara, I shall die if Malcolm MacEwan goes away. I must have been mad. I've almost died of loneliness since I...oh, dear, what have I done? Sara, Felicity, we've got to find Malcolm. I must talk to him."

Abigail sprang up from her chair and frantically paced this way and that, as if looking for an answer. "Maybe I can stop the coach if I cut across the field," she decided.

Sara had a better idea. "He has to go to the general store to catch the coach. Felicity and I will run back and harness the buggy to drive you."

Abigail, pleased that someone else was in control,

agreed. So, having just caught their breaths, Sara and Felicity dashed out the door and ran all the way back home as if their lives depended on it.

The night had not passed well for Janet King. Once the tears had passed, dawn soon followed, and she'd slept fitfully until the morning sun woke her.

When Alec didn't show up for breakfast, she began to fret. Perhaps he had taken her at her word and gone off to see the world. By eight-thirty, she had worked herself into such a terrible state, imagining in great detail all the dreadful things that could have befallen him, that she sent Sara and Felicity to search for him.

When the girls didn't return, she grew concerned and set out to look for him herself. As she rounded the corner of the barn she was met by an absurd sight. There, stretched out on the most beautiful bed she had ever seen, was her husband, as comfy as you please.

"Alec King. What a bed! What's it doing here?"

"You said you liked sleeping in the barn," he drawled.

"I beg your pardon?"

"I never did fix ours, and I saw this at the auction the other day. Malcolm outbid—" He cut himself short, "It's a long story."

"You never said a word about it."

Alec stood up and faced his wife. He looked at her, his eyes full of love.

"I've been forgetting a lot of things lately...especially where you're concerned."

"Well, what a change. It certainly is different from that wobbly old bed of ours," Janet remarked flippantly. Then she dropped her defenses. His words and his look melted her heart.

"Oh, Alec."

Slowly, they moved towards each other. Janet raised her face to Alec who bent down to meet her lips. Unfortunately, their kiss was curtailed by a loud ruckus from the other side of the barn.

Sara had insisted upon hitching up the horse herself, even though she had never done it before in her life. She could be quite bossy when she put her mind to it. Felicity looked on in helpless frustration. Sara's pigheadedness was causing them to lose time.

"It goes in there." Felicity was beside herself with irritation.

"I don't want to put my hand in the horse's mouth." Sara wrinkled up her nose in disgust.

This was not a time for niceties. In utter exasperation, Felicity grabbed the bit from her cousin's hand without so much as a 'by-your-leave.' "You don't have to," she barked. "Let me do it."

"What the dickens are you two up to?" Alec called as he rounded the barn. Two heads turned up at once, annoyed that their efforts were being so rudely delayed. In spite of the interference, Felicity was relieved to see her parents, arm in arm once more.

"Aunt Abigail is beside herself with despair," Sara explained. "It's a matter of life and death." She felt no need to explain the whole story, there was so little time. The beginning and the end would have to do.

"Well, it will be if it's hitched up wrong," Alec warned them.

"It's not," Felicity replied indignantly.

With no time to waste, the girls jumped into the buggy and drove away, still haggling.

"So, you'd like to see Abigail and Malcolm together?" Janet asked coyly, once they were again alone.

"Yes. They deserve each other, like another couple I know."

Alec gazed deeply into her eyes. Janet returned his gaze and wordlessly they confirmed their love. Then the kiss, which had been so impatiently delayed, happily resumed.

Chapter Twenty

Abigail was in a complete tizzy. She just knew some horrible disaster had happened to delay the girls. Every five seconds she would consult her watch. They would never make it in time. Fighting her mounting hysteria, she paced to and fro in front of her white picket fence.

By the time the girls arrived with the buggy, Abigail had worked herself up to a fever pitch. Her ginger hair frizzled out from her head in a great state of agitation. Her gray wool cape was askew, with one side flapped up over her shoulder, exposing its crimson lining. Her hat barely clung to her head and sat at an angle so acute that one inch farther and it would have been on the ground.

When the buggy arrived, she leapt on board before it had even had a chance to stop. With a powerful shove which belied her usual delicacy, Abigail pushed Felicity aside and took the reins.

The horse responded to the urgency of the situation. With a jolt, the buggy pulled away and rattled noisily through the quiet streets of Avonlea.

Mrs. Potts stood by the trim white fence that surrounded the Biggins' house. Mrs. Biggins stood on the other side with her apron on. Mrs. Potts had only just heard the news of the much-expected departure of Malcolm MacEwan, and she wanted to discuss, in gory detail, the whole messy affair. The two friends agreed that it was an outrageous thing for that Abigail Ward to have done. Imagine driving him away for a second time.

At first, they heard what sounded like a mild rumbling, perhaps thunder in the distance. The two good ladies paid it no mind, for nothing as paltry as weather could stop them when there were important matters to discuss. But then it grew louder and louder, until it was fast upon them. Mrs. Potts barely had time to jump out of the way before the reckless buggy came careening past. Holding the reins was Abigail Ward, driving like a woman possessed. The two women watched in amazement. For perhaps the first and only time in her life, Mrs. Potts was speechless.

Mr. Lawson sat on the porch of his general store. He was sorry that Malcolm MacEwan had left. He liked the man. The clatter and bang of the buggy startled him. Abigail Ward, as he had never before seen her, jumped off and addressed him.

"Mr. Lawson," she panted, "have you seen Mr. MacEwan?"

"He left already, Abigail. On the coach, not moments ago."

But before he could even finish, Abigail had raced back to the buggy and sped off like an arrow from a bow. Mr. Lawson shook his head in amazement. Stranger things on heaven and earth...he mused.

Sara and Felicity clung for dear life as their aunt spurred the horse to go faster and faster. At each turn, at every bump, they were convinced the buggy would fly completely out of control, spilling them fatally on to the road. Sara gripped the side of the wagon with such tenacity that her knuckles were white. Felicity was so frightened she had tears in her eyes.

Abigail half stood as she drove. Her expression was wild. Her cape flew straight out behind her like a banner of war. "*Ya!*" she yelled at the horse, snapping the reins. "*Ya, ya!*" Her voice rasped with the effort.

The trees sped by in a blur. Foam flecked the horse's back and its ears flattened against its head. Its muscles strained and its eyes rolled back, but still she urged it on, "*Ya!*"

Malcolm sat in the lonely coach watching the landscape, wishing to imprint the sight on his memory. He drank in and savored the tiniest detail, knowing he was seeing it for the last time.

All that he gazed on—every leaf, every rock, every gentle hill—reminded him of Abigail. In his mind, he could see her. He conjured up her delicate face, the look of love she had turned on him when she'd agreed to be his wife. He could almost hear her sweet voice speaking his name— "*Malcolm.*"

"Malcolm!" a voice screamed through his thoughts. Had his grief driven him mad?

"*Malcolm*," it bawled again. His heart leapt for joy. It was too good to be true.

Malcolm stuck his head out of the coach window. Behind on the road, gaining fast, was a sight for sore eyes. Driving as if her life depended on it and looking as wild as a banshee was his own dear love.

"Driver! Stop the coach!" he ordered.

The coach slowed to a halt. Malcolm's foot touched the ground in time to catch Abigail as she flung herself into his arms.

"Malcolm! Please don't go," she pleaded. "I'll marry you. I'll go anywhere. You can bring as much mud into the house as you want!"

Malcolm held her close. Patting her gently, he comforted her. "There, there. Of course I won't be going, if that's what you want, Abby dear."

"And you'll come back with me right now?"

"Of course. Of course."

Then they kissed. And kissed again. Then, for a third time their lips met. They would have repeated the act any number of times but for a gentle clearing of a throat, coming from the direction of the buggy.

Sara Stanley and Felicity King were seated in the buggy, their expressions slightly jarred. One's face, Malcolm noted, was as white as a freshly laundered sheet. The other's complexion sported an

unusual shade of green. Malcolm smiled at them.
Doffing his hat, he grinned.

"Well, lassies, it looks as though we'll be getting
to know each other a little better."

Abigail smiled at them, her face radiant with
happiness.

"You girls are heaven-sent. How can I ever
thank you?"

"There is one thing you can do, Aunt Abigail,"
Sara said, shakily. "Let Mr. MacEwan drive the
buggy home."

So Mr. MacEwan, a happy man, took the reins
and drove, with extreme care, all the way back to
Avonlea.

The wedding of Malcolm MacEwan and Abigail
Ward took place in late September of that year.
Everyone agreed that it was indeed fortunate that
Abigail hadn't let Malcolm get away this time. Mrs.
Potts, that weather vane of opinion, claimed to
anyone who would care to listen that she knew the
wedding would occur all along.

All who attended had to agree that Abigail
made a lovely bride. The peach of her satin gown
brought out her complexion beautifully. Mrs.
Lawson, her eyes running liberally with joyful
tears, claimed the credit for the fashion success.

Malcolm MacEwan stood proud and tall at the

altar, awaiting the fulfillment of his lifelong dream. All conceded he looked dashing and very refined in his dark, cutaway tailcoat, and his striped cravat. Mr. Lawson informed those who cared to know that it had come from the best tailor in Halifax.

Alec King stood by the groom as his best man, honored to perform the service.

Sara Stanley and Felicity King accompanied their aunt up the aisle and stood proudly by her side as she spoke her vows. It was with some justification that they claimed responsibility for the whole affair. For without their warning and their part in that wild ride, the wedding might never have happened.

❧ ❧ ❧

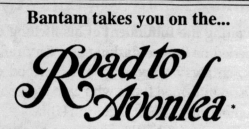

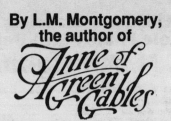